The Bunce

By Michael de Larrabeiti

THE BUNCE
A ROSE BEYOND THE THAMES
THE BORRIBLES
THE REDWATER RAID

The Bunce

MICHAEL DE LARRABEITI

PUBLISHED FOR THE CRIME CLUB BY
DOUBLEDAY & COMPANY, INC.
GARDEN CITY, NEW YORK
1981

No reference is made or intended in this book
to any police officer or group of police officers.
Nothing resembling "The Bunce" exists,
nor is it likely to.
This is just a story.

Library of Congress Cataloging in Publication Data
De Larrabeiti, Michael.
The bunce.
I. Title.
PR6054.E134B8   1981   823'.914
ISBN 0-385-17753-4   AACR2
Library of Congress Catalog Card Number 81-3249

Copyright © 1980 by Michael de Larrabeiti
All Rights Reserved
Printed in the United States of America

For Celia

ACKNOWLEDGEMENTS

I have to thank Bill Johnson of Magic Lantern for allowing me to traduce both him and his company in the interests of *The Bunce*.

My thanks also go to Duncan Nunn and Doug Belassie of The Creative Studio, and to Leslie Eastaugh of Shaw Nichols Associates.

I owe the deepest apologies to "Diver" Jim O'Reilly who, as far as I know, has never been to Oxfordshire.

Contents

Author's Note   1

DAY 11
- *Prologue:* The Soft Touch   3
- *Chapter One:* Billy Jay   8
- *Chapter Two:* Panurge   14
- *Chapter Three:* Billy's Ride   23

DAY 12
- *Chapter Four:* The Morley Way   31
- *Chapter Five:* The Reward   39
- *Chapter Six:* The Morley Show   47
- *Chapter Seven:* Casey Leaves   53
- *Chapter Eight:* Detective-Inspector Fisher   58

DAY 13
- *Chapter Nine:* The Man from the Mirror   64

DAY 14
- *Chapter Ten:* Mr. Nasty   70
- *Chapter Eleven:* Goodbye Eunice   78

DAY 15
- *Chapter Twelve:* A Bumpy Road to Newcastle   84
- *Chapter Thirteen:* The Bunce   92

DAY 16
   Chapter Fourteen: The Show Must Go On   106

DAY 19
   Chapter Fifteen: The Funeral   110

DAYS 19–21
   Chapter Sixteen: Edinburgh/Glasgow   118

DAYS 22–26
   Chapter Seventeen: The Picnic   130

DAYS 27, 28
   Chapter Eighteen: Liverpool   142

DAYS 30–34
   Chapter Nineteen: The Last Show   152

DAY 34
   Chapter Twenty: The Deal   160

DAY 35
   Chapter Twenty-one: The Script   170

bunce, buns, n. (slang) extra gain—used as an interjection
Chambers Twentieth Century Dictionary

bunce (the predominant C.19–20 spelling), bunse, bunt(s). Money: C. 18–early 19. D'Urfey spells it buns. In mid-C. 19–20 it= (costermongers') perquisites; profit; commission; Mayhew spells it bunse and bunts, and pertinently proposes derivation ex sham L. BONUS.
A *Dictionary of Slang and Unconventional English*
Eric Partridge

AUTHOR'S NOTE

Details of robberies committed at Heathrow Airport between October 1972 and March 1976. Information taken from an article in *The Guardian*.

OCTOBER 1972	Platinum, worth	£ 94,837
APRIL 1973	Rough diamonds and platinum, worth	£479,536
FEBRUARY 1975	Platinum plates, worth	£330,831
FEBRUARY 1975	Kruger rands, worth $363,203	£180,000 (approx.)
OCTOBER 1975	Gold bars, worth	£213,996
MARCH 1976	Dollars, Kruger rands, gold bars and gems, worth	£650,000
	TOTAL	£1,949,200

Between the time of the first robbery and the last not one penny of the loot was recovered and not one villain apprehended.

The Guardian article goes on to tell us how the police were at last helped out of their difficulties by a member of the public.

> ... The first major break for police came when Lester Pattinson, an eighteen-year-old athlete from Wandsworth, out for an early morning training run on Putney Heath, saw two men burying some of their loot, including gold coins, two Browning automatic pistols and fifty rounds of ammunition.
>
> Lester Pattinson noted the number of their car and passed it on to the police. They identified the cache as being from Heathrow and arrested the pair, who pleaded guilty to the robbery, which involved £850,000 worth of goods. Dressed as British Airways couriers, the two men

had entered the strongroom, threatened the security guard with an imitation pistol and tied him up.

Working back from this robbery, which took place only a few weeks ago, the police discovered a group of men who had taken part in some five other major thefts at the airport. . . .

The press went mad for Lester Pattinson. Calculating his reward on the usual ten per cent, he stood to get £85,000. Some time later more spoils came to light and it seemed possible that the lucky youth might get as much as £100,000, or even £150,000.

It was a good story and the papers loved it, but the reward was slow in coming, very slow. One year and eight months after the robbery the *Sunday Express* printed this article:

MYSTERIOUS MR. X BLOCKS REWARD FOR LONDON BOY GANGBUSTER

Glowing tributes were paid to Lester Pattinson in court when members of a Heathrow gang were given long jail sentences and he looked forward to receiving the usual ten per cent of the recovered loot. But now, nearly two years after the robbery, twenty-year-old Lester has not received a penny in reward money. For a Mr. X has stepped in and is claiming over half of all the monies. Mystery surrounds Mr. X. Few people know his name, what he does for a living, and what part, if any, he played in smashing the gang of Heathrow robbers. If Mr. X does receive reward money, almost certainly his identity will not be revealed, even to the insurance companies who, anyway, are not obliged to announce publicly how, why, or to whom the money is being paid.

A strange business the reward business.

DAY 11

PROLOGUE

The Soft Touch

The armoured truck rolled into the cargo village that lies on the fringe of Heathrow Airport and halted in front of the Special Merchandise Depot. It was a royal blue truck and had gold portcullises painted on each side. There was a word painted there too, the name of the security firm, Armacor.

The cargo sheds were scrappy; there was plastic and paper litter in the open spaces and dust had drifted into pyramids of dirt in the windless corners behind the buildings. The huts looked like temporary accommodation thrown together for motorway navvies and then abandoned as sub-standard. Their tar-paper roofs were peeling and the cream paint was flaking away from the concrete walls.

No one got out of the truck at first and there was no movement except for the faces, pale and sad beneath black helmets and moving behind the meshed windows. Then, after a moment or two, a big man emerged from the vehicle and stood near it, swinging a night-stick by his side. He was dressed in a dark blue uniform and he wore a tiny portcullis badge on each shoulder. His subordinates called him Commander.

He walked to the front of the truck, looked about him, tapped with his stick and the van reversed up to the double doors of the depot. A plane pulled itself into the sky overhead, but the Commander was used to it and he didn't wince at the noise. When the sound had faded, he took a walkie-talkie from his pocket, spoke into it and the doors of the Special Merchandise Depot were unlocked and a slender man in a soiled airways uniform appeared. On his head was a peaked cap with a hard rim, too large and loose for the skinny skull that carried it. The man's name was Staples; he was near retirement age, no longer strong. His head jerked continually on his yellow neck, the cap not always moving at the same time or in the same direction. He was nervous; behind him in the shed were goods worth upwards of five million pounds; no one knew exactly how much.

The Commander recognised Staples, gave a sign and the truck opened at the rear. Two men jumped down, stretched, and then went into the hut. Another plane took off; gradually the noise of its exhausts died and another noise came in its place: a police siren, hoo-ha, hoo-ha, far away, going fast. The Commander's driver clambered from his cab and strolled over towards Staples. The other Armacor men began to load the truck with heavy black boxes.

The noise of the siren came nearer and suddenly louder, as the police car jumped a rise and showed itself. It was a Range Rover and it was followed by a police Jaguar. Both cars were spotless and their chrome shone in the sunlight. They were moving fast, beautifully driven.

The Range Rover circled and slid to a halt alongside the van. The Jaguar braked, under complete control, skidded a little and stopped so that the back door on the nearside came to rest only inches from the Commander's stomach, giving him no time to move. The door opened unhurriedly and a policeman stood up between the Commander and the car, his suit crumpled and shiny. He had a bullet head, greasy blond hair and a thin face with a thin moustache. He held his warrant card between the first two fingers of his right hand, put his elbow on the open door of his Jaguar and rested it there.

The Commander read the words aloud, "Detective-Inspector Rosser."

"Everything all right?" asked the policeman.

"Yes, why, is there any trouble?"

"Every bloody day . . . the question is . . . is there any trouble here?"

The Commander looked inside the car; two uniformed men, they yawned. The car radio said something. The policemen in the Range Rover stayed where they were and lit cigarettes.

Rosser stared at the Commander. "I had a whisper that some of the lads were going to take something out of here today, dressed as employees of Armacor, you wouldn't do a thing like that, would you?"

The Commander produced his identification. Rosser smiled and waved it away. "That's all right, I recognise you, got your picture somewhere, it's your men I want to check over. Do you know them all? Haven't got one or two new ones with you today, anything of that sort?"

The Commander said, "I know 'em all, each 'n every, as well as I know anyone."

Rosser's smile slid down his face. "That's just it, isn't it? We never really know anyone, do we? Nothing's what it seems and nobody what they pretend."

"Do you know about our cargo?" asked the Commander.

Rosser began to walk towards the shed, "Yes," he said.

Inside the shed it was dark. A yellow light gleamed in the security area and that was all. Staples was standing by an open door watching the Armacor men take heavy black boxes from a large stack. Rosser went over to him and stared carefully into the old man's face. "At least I know you," he said.

"Oh, do you?" said Staples, sniffing his head down into his collar like a tortoise, his cap bouncing on the sides of his skull. "So do lots of people, sunshine, but I don't know you."

"My God, but there's an awful lot of stuff in here," said the Commander. The policeman answered him so carelessly that it was the same as being ignored. "Got the place sealed off by a bloody regiment," he said.

It was then that it happened, and the Commander felt that he was the only person in the world who could see it. Everything slowed down until it stopped completely—until it came to look like a faded black and white still outside the cinema of his boyhood, where the rain water always got in and buckled the photos and discoloured them. He saw two of his men motionless inside the security room, their hands imprisoned in the tight handles of a bullion box. They were staring towards the main doors. The Commander turned and saw that all the policemen were in the hut now, so was the driver and his guard. He noticed that the policemen carried automatics and that his Armacor men were handcuffed.

The Commander raised his chin; he had to, Rosser had placed a gun at his neck and it pointed upwards to his brain.

The policeman said, "I don't want to hurt anyone, I shan't strike you or anything like that, but I will kill you. This is a Browning automatic and it is loaded."

"We're all bona-fide Armacor employees," said the Commander.

"I believe you," said Rosser, "now put your hands behind your back."

The Commander did as he was told. "You can't be coppers, coppers aren't armed."

"They are these days," said Rosser.

"Telephone the office," begged the Commander, "they'll tell you we're straight."

Rosser didn't answer; the handcuffs went on, warm from his pocket.

The two Armacor men still stood inside the security room holding the heavy box; no one had told them what to do. Staples stood by the open door, he seemed a little peeved at being ignored and was not a bit surprised that the Commander had gone crooked. He made way for the two policemen as they passed him to take the bullion box from the security men. He watched complacently as they were handcuffed together. Then one of the policemen said, "Get your hands behind you, old man." He sounded American, and he was polite, like a tourist asking the way.

The Soft Touch

Staples was astounded. "Don't be silly," he spluttered. "I work here, your boss recognised me, he said so."

The policeman touched Staples on the nose with the end of his gun.

"You can't do this," said Staples, without thinking. He struck Rosser petulantly on the shoulder. It was the only violence of the afternoon, and it was a blow meant more to gain attention than to inflict injury. "I'm not scared of you lot . . . those guns are fakes, I bet. Japanese replicas."

Rosser smiled. "Shut up Staples," he said, "or I'll shoot your bloody knee-cap off with a Japanese replica bullet."

Staples was handcuffed and he and the Armacor men were forced to lie full-length on the floor. The policemen loaded what remained of the bullion boxes and Rosser selected certain small packages from those awaiting collection.

"You leave them diamonds," shouted Staples. As he spoke, it dawned on him that these men weren't policemen; that in fact the Commander had been straight all along. He shook his head. "How do you ever know," he asked himself, "when a copper's really a copper?"

Before they went, the policemen cut the telephone wire and gagged their prisoners. The Commander was last; he looked up at Rosser, ashamed of his defeat. "You bastard," he said, "you bastard. You've taken two million quid's worth out of here."

"Oh, at least," said Rosser, "at least."

The policemen left then, closing and locking all doors behind them. They took the police cars and the Armacor security truck, fully loaded, and drove slowly away in the direction of the Stardust Hotel, Heathrow.

CHAPTER ONE

Billy Jay

Billy was in the Stardust Hotel that day and I was there with him.

When you called Billy Jay a lunatic he just grinned, it was his way of admitting it. Billy was a big man, too big to live with. He was six and a half feet tall, with a wide stomach that leant out over a leather belt and pulled the rest of his body along, making the feet run. That gut led Billy by the nose. His face was bizarre, the size and shape of a football on its side, and straw-coloured hair swept his shoulders. He had a big mouth and he could stick a great grin on to it and make it work. It was the grin of a boy caught scrumping the reddest plums in the orchard, yet all the time knowing that he was too young and too lovable to be punished.

Billy was about forty and should have known better but never bothered. The light that flickered in his eyes was a lunatic light, right enough, and it was powered by a thriftless energy. He had strong shoulders and the thighs of a giant. He was a man who could seize little men by their shirt fronts and dangle them in the air.

Billy argued all the time, and although he was continually threatening to hit people he only ever shook them. He was child-like, exasperating and exhausting. In Billy's house doors slammed, voices rose and people left for ever—only to come back the next day. Fran, Billy's wife, had left him a hundred times. She said that living with Billy was like giving up smoking.

He dressed cleanly, fresh jeans and shirts every day; for meetings he wore smart loose suits. He had big feet; his hands were big and he had big dreams. His mind had the eagerness of a bullock; he didn't mean any harm but he used to run at you, knocking you down into the mud and it hurt when you didn't get out of the way.

Going to work with Billy was always frightening, you never knew what might happen. First thing in the morning he hauled you from sleep and threw clothes at your head. He thrust breakfast into your stomach and stuffed money into your pocket. Billy lifted you and his camera gear into the Volvo shooting-brake and aimed it into the middle of the road and he stayed there, defeating traffic by ignoring it, grinning through the windscreen.

The car was part of Billy and it carried everything: a telephone, cassette recorders, dictaphone machines, movie cameras, still cameras, radios, walkie-talkies and booze. Billy started drinking at eleven o'clock in the morning on ordinary days, litre bottles of wine, white or red, it didn't matter. He drank it carelessly, so that the juice ran down his chin and shirt as he drove, empties clinking between the seats. At most meals he ate steak, steak an inch thick and hardly cooked. When he laid a knife across his meat it spurted blood.

He liked his women fashionable, good-looking, big-bosomed and middle-classed, but above all he admired style. What he meant by style in a woman was merely something she had that made other men look at her and envy Billy. It didn't matter what that something was. He made love noisily, trying to bend the woman in half, and the bed under her, laughing in his throat.

There was no inbetween with such a man, you either loved him or you hated him. You went out to do a day's filming with Billy, just for the wages, and you ended up with a part in a French farce or a Greek tragedy. He was a good employer if you could stand it; generous, lovable, impossible to live with. Time spent with him was like being in a room with no door, while a monster smashed the furniture and threw it at you, piece by piece.

In the early days Billy was engaged in freelance filming; documentaries and adverts for television. There came a time when the work dropped off because Billy frightened television people, especially those with thin blood—and that's most of them. Billy went through a hard time and, against his will, was forced away from films and into the A-V business. A-V means audio-visual.

He began by organising trade fairs and then moved into business conferences. He formed a new company, his third, called it Magic Lantern Road Shows, and discovered that he possessed a special talent for disguising other people's shortcomings. He began to make a lot of money and everyone working for him made a lot of money too.

If you took the trouble to ask Billy why he worked at such a rate, and all the time, he would look at you perplexed, as if such a question were unreasonable as well as sacrilegious.

He sometimes said that he meant to be a millionaire by the time he was forty-five. He wanted to make enough money to retire on, to stop working and take it easy; as if Billy Jay could take it easy. I've never seen him sit down with a friend, just to relax, or read a book, alone, under a pool of light in a corner; and I've never seen him stay in one room when he could get up and go out of it.

There was another reason he gave for wanting money, a more secret reason. He wanted, he said, to produce good films of his own instead of the normal crap he did every day. But that was only part of the real answer.

Billy was impressed by conspiracy theories, he collected them. All the half-baked magazine articles he'd ever read on the subject had combined to form a lump of raw thought that lay in his mind like a slab of liver.

The Protocols of the Elders of Zion had been made for him. "It's so obvious," he always said, "so logical. Look at all the trouble they've caused through the centuries, look how much power they've accumulated, communications especially. If they want a film to take off it takes off, and if they don't, it stays in the can."

Sometime later Billy discovered the Illuminati and his mind exploded.

The Illuminati, so he told me, were a sect who ran international politics and had done for centuries. Marx had been one of their tools, so had Napoleon and Bismark. "Don't you see," Billy always insisted, "the Illuminati make the Elders of Zion look like a Tupperware party. You can't play with the Conspiracy, it's too serious; they're into everything, banks, multi-nationals, oil."

According to Billy's theory, everything fell into the province of a secret few and it was they who dictated what we did and what we thought. Their power was eternal, but Billy wasn't going to let them rule him. He would get free of "them" by joining "them," and the only way of joining was by invitation—and guess who were invited? The rich and the powerful. There lay Billy's real ambition, to escape restraint. He knew he had a lot to offer; his brain, his energy, his talent. Meanwhile, he was being wasted. He was cramped by a lack of wealth.

He had to get rich, and getting rich for him tied in with the making of films. Good films, he thought, would make big money; the trouble was that to make the films you needed the money first. "I've got to get there," he used to say, "I don't want to die a worm, I'm better than that, I've got to get out of the ruck. That's reasonable enough, isn't it?"

So Billy ran everywhere, worked all the time, earnt heaps of money and then spent it on things like mortgages and mistresses, food and drink, cars. His overdraft grew like honeysuckle over everything he did, and it always stood near the twenty or thirty grand mark. Billy was a big power-station glowing in the sky, day and night, burning coal to make electricity, using the electricity to dig the coal. Billy got older and his dream stayed beyond the reach of his arm.

And so Billy Jay threw himself into the A-V game, bringing enthusiasm, knowledge and imagination into a business that badly needed it. Conferences had been dull affairs, but not after Billy came along; he changed all that.

An A-V production cannot exist without several tons of equipment: electric cables, amplifiers and scores of projectors, both movie and still. It also needs thousands of colour slides, especially created for rippling across enormous screens to the accompaniment of well-chosen music. Such a show calls for tape-decks, decoders, conference rooms big enough for trucks to drive into, and crazy technicians who don't mind working a month of sleepless weeks when they must.

I don't work for Billy full-time, but then I don't work for anyone full-time. When I can afford to, I put my feet up and do nothing for as long as the money lasts. When it has gone, I work for any A-V firm that will pay me. I drive vans, I run cable, I stage-manage, I help build the sets too, and I often write the scripts. "The Wordsmith," Billy calls me.

I started work, straight from school, as a messenger with a documentary film company in Wardour Street, but even then I had a hatred of regular work. I earnt good money and no doubt could have made something of myself, but I didn't. It was something to do with the people around me, seeing them cheated out of their personalities, swindled out of life by a career. They behaved as if that was all there was. I wanted something more, something less. I was greedy.

At the beginning, like everyone else, I had thought the film industry glamorous, but it wasn't. It was as false and as boring as any other job; the same old people I didn't want to spend my life with. I soon decided that there was nothing better than not working, and that what I wanted was no dedication and no life's work.

But I still had to earn my bread, so I went where the money was, freelancing for Billy and the others who ran firms like his. I drove round the country, worked hard when I had to, drank a lot, fell into bed with women whenever there was an offer and whatever they looked like. As far as I was concerned, it could have gone on for ever. It didn't, we became involved in one of the Heathrow robberies. And worse, we ran into the Bunce. But before the Bunce came the Morley show; there couldn't have been one without the other.

DAY 11

CHAPTER TWO

Panurge

The Stardust Hotel, Heathrow, is a triangular lump of concrete with slots for windows. It has no face and no back and stands in a strip of emptiness between the airport and the motorway. Under the ground are three platforms of garaging, and the hotel sits above looking in at itself. It is a hotel you cannot walk to; as a guest, you drive underneath the building and keep going until you run out of road. You leave your car in the dark, ride upwards in a lift and, when the door opens, you find yourself beneath a heavy canopy of colour and music, quarantined in comfort.

It was lunchtime and we sat in the darkness of the conference room, as long as a football pitch it was, and looked at the set. Three of us sat on tilted chairs, backs against the back wall; Billy, Duggie and me. We had been up all day and all night—and the night before that too. We'd been drinking, we had splinters, broken fingernails, red eyes; and we wanted to go to bed. Our client was Morley Products (America) Incorporated, and it was the biggest show that Billy had ever tackled. The whole circus was costing five million dollars, and Billy's end of it was worth £90,000.

It was lunchtime, but there in the dark it felt like the middle of the night. It always felt like the night; we worked in the dark all the time, judging the quality of the slides, keeping the focus crisp. We hadn't seen daylight for a fortnight, getting the show to run, changing the script. Now the set was finished and the riggers were sleeping at last, nine or ten of them if you counted their women, women in ethnic clothes and sandals. The riggers shifted the show whenever Billy said, drinking, smoking pot and sleeping anywhere, underneath the stage mostly.

Our set was a stretch of England's green and pleasant land, canvas on a wood and metal frame, painted. It came to pieces in twenty-three large sections and was designed to fit into the riggers' pantechnicon. Stage right was a small church with a real pulpit on the outside, facing the audience. Rolling fields in perspective led away from the church and drew the eye to haystacks, hedges, trees and bushes; a gentle eighteenth-century landscape.

Spreading above and behind everything was a sky made of five six-by-six screens which were to carry the visualisation of the Morley message. Stage left was a small thatched cottage, modelled on Anne Hathaway's. In the cottage was a door, and performers and speakers could reach the stage here or cross to the pulpit. There was a long castellated wall too, and in the middle of it a wide drawbridge. Across the stage ran the moat, real water in a plastic ditch; stage right it tumbled prettily down some painted rocks into a pool and was returned stage left in a pipeline, electrically pumped without a sound. "First time it's ever been done," Billy told his visitors.

The show carried a mass of lighting. Whole banks of colour climbed the walls behind the set and there were scores of lamps concealed in every corner of the conference room. At the end of the show they would all burn up together, slowly, trained on the screens, on the ceilings and on the walls. There would be a blaze of power over the whole room and flaming words would spread across the sky. "Nature will love you if you will love her." It was called the Morley Dawn.

We sat there. Duncan was on the back projection rostrum pressing buttons, while the three of us checked the slides as they appeared. "Diver" Jim was just visible on the balcony behind his light control panel. Lights both front and back of the set were his; light rising, light falling, glowing and whirling, stars in the roof, spots on the speakers, limes on the performers, all were his. When the presentation reached its climax, it was Jim who manufactured the Morley Dawn.

We came to the last slide. "Okay," said Billy, and Duncan cut the power and the screen went black.

"House," I shouted, and Jim brought the house lights up to half. Duncan appeared on stage, crossed the foot-bridge that spanned the moat, jumped into the auditorium and then began the long walk down the hall to join us.

A waitress pushed backward through a door and brought a shaft of brighter light with her. She was carrying a large tray of drinks to half a dozen reporters sitting between us and the screen. They had already drunk enough. One of them swivelled loosely in his chair and waved at us. "Great," he shouted, "really great."

Billy yelled, "Yeah," and waved back, smiling as if to a foreigner. And then he said, for only us to hear, "What a bitch!" As the waitress went to leave he called to her.

She came and stood by us, disapproving, we weren't real hotel people; our clothes were dirty and she knew we spat on the carpet. Billy gave her a pound note and she looked embarrassed.

"Sweetheart," he said. "I want five gin and tonics." The waitress turned to go but Billy leant forward and placed his hand on her back, just where it sloped out to become a skinny buttock. His hand was enormous there, you could imagine Billy picking the woman up and biting her head away at the neck, the way kids eat jelly-babies.

"When I say a gin and tonic I mean a gin and tonic, in a pint mug, half gin, half tonic, lots of ice and lemon. The pound is for you, the drinks go on the Morley account." The waitress nodded and went through the nearest door. Duncan reached us and sat down.

"Do you think she understood?" he said.

"I dunno," said Billy, "they're all Portuguese." Then he shouted, "Come on down, Jim, drinks."

A woman's laugh rose from the journalists. Some men laughed with her and she stood up and we saw her raise a glass and say something we couldn't hear. She turned her head in our direction and looked across the crescents of chairbacks. She was looking at Billy. He knew she was and he let the front legs of his chair come softly down to the carpet. "I want that," he said.

Casey Roberts was a freelance who wrote informative articles for the women who read the Sunday newspapers. She was intelligent and she was popular. When you first met her she made sure that she gave you an impression of dedicated carelessness. A little later you realised that this affectation, if it was an affectation, hid the working of a busy mind, preoccupied mainly with Casey Roberts, her work and its excellence. She was unfair; she had confidence and money. She was as small-boned and slight as Billy was big. The idea of them making love together seemed to pose a number of technical problems, even for the imagination of "Diver" Jim, who sat down with us in time to hear what Billy had said. He raised his eyebrows. "She's too small and too smart for you, Billy."

Billy shoved his chair back against the wall. "They all go," he said, "all of them."

We had met Casey right at the beginning. She'd been researching an article on the Morley operation and that had brought her to the Magic Lantern Studios. She'd finished her piece but had stayed on to investigate the conference business and how it worked. During the long run-up to the show, we had come to know her well and she seemed easy to know at first. She looked at you hard and put all the frankness she could into her eyes. I found it disturbing—so much frankness there that I wondered if there was any truth. I've always distrusted journalists as a race; all that energy, all that involvement and self-righteousness. Only Casey seemed special and I exonerated her.

There are some women who talk to men the way one man

talks to another, not letting their sexuality get in the way. Casey talked to you like that, and at the same time she brandished her sexuality at you like a cutlass. It was a kind of contempt she had. There wasn't two-pennyworth of her and yet she could tear a man apart like he was half a pint of shrimps. Delicate and good-looking, she knew it. At first I thought she wasn't a snob in any sense. Later on I didn't know, but I enjoyed being in her company and reserved my dislike.

She intrigued Billy too. Casey had more style than any other woman he'd met; he couldn't stop staring at her. We all knew it was going to happen, even Fran, Billy's wife, she knew too.

Billy thought that if he could possess Casey, just once, he could possess her style. It was the old cannibal theory of eating the best people so that you could acquire their qualities, their bravery, their intelligence and their wit. Billy was a sexual cannibal. Casey had a real working mind, she had been finely educated and she had a wonderful body. Billy longed to go to bed with her for all the usual reasons, but more than that he thought that by doing so he would gain an honorary Ph.D. That day, Day 11 on the Morley schedule, Billy wanted to sleep with Casey Roberts more than he wanted anything else in the world. I understood those feelings because I desired her just as much as he did. What I couldn't understand was why she should sleep with Billy, because it was obvious that she was going to.

The sallow-skinned waitress came back with our pints of gin and tonic and Billy ordered some more. We drank slowly, getting ready for sleep, and we stared at the group of men where Casey sat. I glanced at Billy's face; he was exhausted but his eyes flared up at the woman. He turned and caught me looking at him.

"You'd better get some sleep," he said, "all of you, right away. I want you back down here by nine tonight, we've got to run through the whole thing."

"How long, rehearsals?" That was Jim.

"If it goes well, we'll be back in bed by midnight."

The blond head of Casey rose from the cluster of dark lounge suits. Billy rose too.

"I'll see you at nine," he said, putting down his glass and moving towards the edge of the room to intercept Casey, who was leaving the men, drinks lolling in their fingers and their eyes on her behind.

They met in the aisle near the door, Billy leant against the wall and his grin shone in the half-light.

"He can't take her to his room," I said, "Fran's bringing some slides from the office."

Casey stood side by side with Billy and they gazed in our direction but with their eyes focused somewhere else. She smiled and moved her head as Billy spoke, tossing her hair when he made her laugh. It was his eagerness, someone like Casey would see Billy coming a mile off, his tail went up on the horizon. After a minute or two, they went through the door together.

Our waitress came back and put some more drinks on the table.

"*Muchas gracias*," said Duggie with bitterness, but the waitress didn't notice it and hung on a foot for a moment, smiling, to see if he was going to say anything else. Duggie didn't and she went away.

I stood up. "I'll be back in a minute."

Duncan said, "Where are you going?"

"I'm going to see what they're up to, you know Billy and his stories, I want to know if he really does it."

"You're a shit," said Duggie, and he meant it. We didn't get on all that well.

Outside the conference room, in a corridor leading to reception, was a row of lifts with bright steel doors. I got into the corridor in time to see a set of them closing on Billy and Casey, standing to face each other, holding both hands and smiling, then they were gone. I looked at the row of green figures above my head, the lift was going down to the garages.

Another lift came and it opened automatically. It knew

what I wanted and it was empty. I stepped in and pressed a transparent perspex square which had the figure three on it. That was the lowest section of the garage and our truck was parked there, by the ramp near the goods lift.

The lift, my lift, hit the bottom level and, as the doors peeled into their recesses, I leant to one side and kept my finger on the Doors Open button.

The garage was huge, grey and concrete, lit from overhead with fluorescent rods, and in the places where there should have been shadows there were just cold oblongs of mauve, trying to dull the gleaming chrome of parked cars. There were car shapes too, covered in grey plastic sheeting, vehicles left behind for weeks while their owners flew away to the sun and the sea. Huge ribbed pillars made a labyrinth of the place and held the hotel up in the air.

Billy walked down the wide road of the garage, staggering a little as he went. He had solved one of the technical problems already. He was carrying Casey like a child, her legs round his waist, his hands under her buttocks, mouth on mouth. Further down the garage I could see our three-tonner, it was white and carried on its sides, in sepia lettering, our banner: The Magic Lantern Road Show. On the ramp leading to the goods lift stood another three-tonner, nothing to do with us but I noticed the coincidence. It was green and it belonged to Phillip's Frozen Foods—The Best.

When Billy reached our van he lowered Casey to the ground, unlocked the slatted roller at the back and let it wind up on its spring. It made a lot of noise. He lifted the woman into the van and she went out of sight. Reaching forward, Billy pulled out a length of plastic piping, it was pretty long and it had a hand pump in the middle of it. It was his syphon gadget.

Billy stole petrol whenever he could; he hated paying for it, it was one of his things. The van next to ours, on a slightly elevated level, was too much of a temptation. If he hadn't been half drunk, if he hadn't wanted to show off to Casey, he wouldn't have done it and the lives of three people would have been saved. Neither Billy, nor I as I watched him, knew what he was getting us into. I lifted my finger from the button. The lift doors closed and I rode upwards.

Ken Hutchins had done the conversion on Billy's van in the backyard of the Magic Lantern studios. It had taken him about a month of evenings. Ken was carpenter, painter, decorator and builder. He was slow, talkative and friendly, and he built like he talked, thoroughly.

He had redesigned the truck so that it could carry our machines securely clipped into racks and shelves. Everything slotted into its appointed place. The van was widely admired as a masterpiece but Ken had lavished most of his time and all his leisurely skill on fitting out the "luton."

"The luton," he told me, "is that part of the truck that comes out over the cab of some lorries, a rectangular space, sometimes as long as eight or ten feet, you know, four or five feet wide, high enough to kneel in. A useful space and very often a space that is wasted, entirely—but not in this case, not in this case. I suppose the name comes from the town Luton, I mean they do make a lot of vehicles in Luton . . ."

Magic Lantern did a lot of miles in the year, and Billy had Ken make a bedroom in the luton, big and comfortable, so that at least one member of the crew could sleep as we drove from venue to venue. It wasn't just a question of throwing a mattress in there, Billy had to have all the bits and pieces, all the gadgets.

A lined door on overheard hinges sealed the luton off from the body of the truck. Another flap had been let into the side so that we could get in and out even when the van was fully loaded. In the front of the luton were ventilation grilles and a plate-glass porthole, disguised from the outside by the Magic Lantern lettering. The installation was immensely comfortable; a double mattress, a duvet, pillows, a bedside light, a bookshelf with paperbacks, a small fridge with gin and tonic in it, and an intercom connected to the cab.

Ken had worked hard, and when he'd finished the van and

the sign-writing he christened it Panurge and printed the name, small, in a corner at the front. Every time Billy, or any other member of the road show scored in the luton, Ken stood on the bonnet and painted a tiny swastika by the van's name. When Billy Jay and Casey Roberts climbed in there that afternoon, Panurge had already registered twenty-five hits, only two of them mine.

I came out of the lift and went to recover my pint of gin and tonic. Duncan, Duggie and Jim had gone. I took my drink, and Billy's, to my room, pulled the curtains, switched on the colour television and, with the remote control switch, I flipped the vision round and round the four films which the hotel had on offer. I sipped my drink and waited for sleep, but it was a long time coming. It was difficult not to think of Billy and Casey and what they were doing. But whatever they did, I knew Billy would tell me afterwards, and in great detail.

DAY 11

CHAPTER THREE

Billy's Ride

Casey was naked on the mattress by the time Billy appeared over the tailboard. He pulled the shutter down, making the inside of the van greenish and secret, then he stripped, skimming his clothes into a pile beyond the girl, his limbs gleaming in the half-light like fish in a dark pool. He swung up beside her and lowered the long flap that sealed off the luton, its perfect fit providing him with a feeling of smugness and security. Casey and he were alone in that strange bed, locked in the luton of a three-ton truck at the bottom of a garage under the Stardust Hotel, Heathrow.

"Billy," she said, "you smell of petrol."

"I know," he raised his head to look at her. "I just nicked a tankful."

In a little while they made love and then they fell asleep. Billy slept well, he always did, but when he came to he realised, in the same moment, that the noise that had roused him had come from outside the van. Casey was on her left side, her right buttock curving up sharply from the mattress. Her body was warm and Billy touched it as he leant over to look through the plate-glass porthole.

The sound came again; the scrape of tyres. Two police cars swept into the garage, a Range Rover and a Jaguar, slammed by their drivers over the ramps that were meant to slow them down. Once more the tyres scraped; the cars reversed into vacant slots and four uniformed policemen came out of them and began to cover both vehicles in plastic sheeting bearing the name of the hotel. Billy saw a fifth man in plain clothes leave the others and go towards the Phillip's Frozen Food truck. A second later it rolled down the goods ramp under its own weight and stopped between Panurge and the police cars. Everything happened very quickly but no one hurried.

Billy guessed that something was up and he was not surprised when the policemen began pulling off their uniforms to reveal casual clothing underneath, but he was perturbed to see that they were wearing shoulder holsters with automatics in them.

The Armacor truck was opened and the four men began shifting a large number of black boxes over to the Phillip's lorry where the man at the wheel touched the ignition and the engine fired. The motor ran easily, it had been well looked after.

Billy closed his eyes and lowered his head and wondered how much petrol he had left in the tank. Not much. He looked out again. The man in the cab bent to check the fuel gauge, making sure. He had a hard face, and his blond hair was cut short to the side of his head. His suit was ordinary and shiny.

He leapt from the cab. "Hang on," he shouted, "some bastard's had our petrol."

Casey turned in her sleep, moved her legs, opened her eyes, then closed them again. Billy pulled the duvet back to her shoulder and put a pillow over her head and she slept on.

He waited, scared. Billy could handle himself in the average fight but he had no special training, none at all. It could not have been worse; there were five of them, armed. He'd stolen their petrol and he was naked.

Someone climbed into Panurge. Billy flicked a switch and the microphone in the cab came live just in time for him to hear a jangling as the someone looked for a key that would work the ignition. The key turned, the engine fired, revved hard to test its condition, to see how far the petrol marker would float. There was a cursing from below; whoever it was had guessed where his petrol had gone.

Panurge was moved forward and loaded. From the porthole, Billy saw four men get into a family saloon, blue. It pulled ahead out of the garage, the van following along the descending curve of road which led from the hotel to the crowded lanes of the M4 motorway, the best place in the world to hide a lorry.

Billy leant over and opened the fridge and took out a fresh quart of gin, a tonic bottle and two tumblers. No sound came through the speaker from below, the driver was alone. Billy was not worried about being discovered, there was six inches of daylight between the bottom of the luton and the roof of the cab. He nudged Casey awake and she sat up. "We're moving," she said.

Billy sniggered and poured them both a strong drink. "The man whose van I nicked the petrol from has come along, in a hurry, and nicked my van, and we're still in it."

"You've got to be joking."

"I'm not," said Billy, "and they have guns and they aren't joking either. They've just done something very big and you'd better believe it."

"Just sit here until they go away?"

"I'm not taking on the five of them, and neither are you." Billy clenched his fist and placed it under Casey's chin.

She raised her glass an inch towards Billy and rested her teeth on the rim of it, considering his advice. Then she said, "I want a pee."

Billy closed his eyes in anger, but at the same moment he realised that he needed one too. "You'll have to sit on it," he said, "unless I can think of something." He opened the fridge door and took out a large plastic container, which was used for keeping salads fresh on long trips. He pulled the lid off and handed it over. "There you go," he said, placing his oval head on one side, "use that."

"What about you?" asked Casey.

Billy laughed. "If we drink enough I can use the gin bottle."

The motorway is one long place and it is a place that Billy knows inside out, up and down. Billy loves the highway; it is fast and modern, it works well and it's big enough for him. The motorway is Billy's favourite gadget. In the A-V business we spend half our time driving on it and watching the slabs of concrete zip away beneath our feet. It is the all sitting, all moving show; millions of people passing each other and never meeting except in accident and blood.

Panurge rolled westward along the M4, keeping well below the speed limit; and Billy knew where he was all the time. Casey and Billy squatted on the mattress, still naked, and waited. She sat cross-legged; demi-lotus with gin. There was nothing much to do and they were both of them scared of what might happen if they were found. They drank and listened to the noise of the motorway.

The car turned off towards Newbury and the van followed. Billy gazed through the porthole, noting every change of direction until they came to the village of Waddestone, and then he stopped bothering. He'd shot a commercial in Waddestone once, using its pretty main street and thatched cottages as the background for some "country fresh" face cream.

Panurge was driven past the church, past the school, and half a mile further on they came to a large house, built of sandstone and standing in its own grounds. There was a rear entrance with a drive that led between high hedges. The van was reversed into darkness and garage doors were closed on it. Billy rolled over on the mattress, slid open a grating and peered into the back of the truck.

There was little to see. Someone threw up the steel shutter, the springs of the van gave a little when two men jumped aboard to unload, passing the bullion boxes down to their three colleagues. The men hardly spoke and, when they did, Billy could sense both relief and excitement in their voices. The accents were American except for the man with greasy blond hair. He was smiling and cheerful and his pleasure made his face less forbidding, but then all of them looked content; richer and wiser men.

Billy feared at first that the van would be locked in the garage overnight, but things didn't turn out that way. As soon as the unloading had been completed, the van was driven from the garage, through the village and across the motorway.

"We're on the north side of the M4," said Billy, and he and Casey stretched under the duvet and warmed their bodies. Out over the six lanes of traffic, the sun was going down and the horizon was already dark. Casey flung her arms around Billy's wobbling belly and pulled him on top of her.

It was late when the van stopped. The cab door slammed, there were footsteps and a car stopped nearby, another door slammed, the car drove away and there was quietness.

Billy looked through the porthole; a spacious residential street, a tarred and gravelled road with a steep camber, distant lamp posts and the shapes of lumpy Victorian houses set well back from the pavements, secure behind square lawns.

"We've been dumped," he said, "dumped I don't know where."

Casey shoved her face beside Billy's and looked out. "It's just like Oxford," she said. "It is Oxford, I used to have digs near here when I was at Somerville."

"Somerville," said Billy pleased. "That's nice, sounds like a bloody cocoa."

They dressed and scrambled down onto the road. Billy went straight to the cab and pulled open the door. Nothing had been left behind, it was as if the whole thing had never happened. Casey walked up the street to look for a nameplate.

Billy snatched up his phone and pressed the button on the dashboard. When he heard the voice of the operator, he said, "Find the number of the Stardust Hotel, Heathrow, and put me through. This is 07 4611."

The hotel answered and Billy asked for Duncan, because Duncan has the reputation of being a calm and equable person, but when Duncan went on the line he wasn't calm at all. "Where the hell have you been?" he said.

Duncan's voice was thin over the radio but it was very angry, I know it was angry because I was sitting next to him as he took the call. We'd just finished the full run-through of the show, with Max breathing down our necks and asking every five seconds where Billy had got to. Max was our client, the Morley man.

"I'm sorry," said Billy, aiming a lot of contrition into the receiver.

The anger went out of Duncan and he gave in. After all, we were in it together, weren't we, all the time? Though it was true that we were often quarrelsome, it was not with each other so much as with the work, with the crap we had to swallow. Didn't our favourite punch line come from the joke where hell was neck high in shit, and the new arrival thought it wasn't too bad until the Devil told him that the tea break was over and it was time for all sinners to get back on their heads? Every show, as Duncan pressed the button that would roll the rubbish forward, we said it to each other: "Okay, fellas, back on your heads."

Duncan laughed, "The rehearsal was fine," he said, "cues fine, music fine, they heard everything, saw everything, one or two mistakes, nothing we can't sort out in the morning."

"Was Max really angry?"

"Mike told him that you'd had to go and save a show in Liverpool . . . what really happened to you?"

"I was in the luton and someone drove off with it, really, I was shanghaied."

Billy put so much energy into his stories that by the time he'd finished telling you one it was true; he'd been mugged by ten blokes, he'd been directed onto the wrong train, run out of petrol on Dartmoor, in a snowdrift; beautiful stories, tall as telegraph poles, incredible as Christmas.

"Why didn't you shout at them through the mike?" asked Duncan. "That would have scared them."

"They were armed," Billy said, "I'm no hero."

"That's right, Billy, you aren't. When are you coming back?"

"Later on, I might as well eat here now."

"Where?"

"I think it's Oxford, but I'm not sure yet."

"Shall I tell that to Fran, if she rings? He thinks he's in Oxford but he doesn't know yet."

"Piss off," said Billy. "Tell her what you told Max. I'll see you tomorrow." He threw the receiver down.

There was no sign of Casey. He looked along the road, peering into a dark yellow puddle of light that lay further away down the street. Nothing. He heard a noise from behind the van and, walking round, he came upon her closing the slatted shutter.

"I'm hungry," said Billy. "I want three steaks, four litres of wine and five rum babas. Where are we?"

"It's Oxford, all right," said Casey.

"Oxford, The Randolph, they'll take credit cards."

"Hotels, cheque cards," said Casey, "that's all you think of. I know where the meat is raw and the brandy is older than you are."

Billy locked the back of the truck.

"I like your lorry," said Casey watching. "I've never had a man in a luton before . . . The Luton Club . . . everyone's done it in Concorde."

"Standing up in a canoe?"

"Of course, but not for long."

With a feeling of real affection, Billy pulled the woman to him, lifted her bodily by the elbows and kissed her as softly as he knew how, like a boy on his first date. When Casey was standing on the road again, she pushed him away.

"Get in the van, Billy, I'll take you to dinner."

Billy turned but she touched him on the arm. "Don't go thinking I'm yours now," she said, "just because of that. I'm nobody's."

Casey had sensed already what we all knew about Billy. He had an eagerness to fall in love, he needed to, as often as he could, deeply, concocting the passion within himself if he had to. The sex was extra.

"Don't you try to fall in love with me," she added, "I don't want it."

Billy forced a laugh. "I haven't got the time," he said, "I've got a fortune to make."

They climbed into the van then, and he drove it into the Banbury road and turned left.

"Just drive where I tell you," said Casey, and she wound down the window and flicked her cigarette at the passing pavement, expertly, like a lorry driver's mate. A police car overtook them at speed, its blue light spinning.

"Are you going to tell the fuzz what happened?" she asked.

"You must be joking," said Billy, "I hope those guys get away with it."

DAY 12

CHAPTER FOUR

The Morley Way

I awoke the next morning in 3321. It was early and I gazed for a long while at the ceiling. I couldn't see it because I'd pulled the curtains on going to bed so that the daylight wouldn't wake me. It didn't matter, I knew all the colours in the room: cream walls, dark brown coverlet on the couches, white furniture, beige bath, beige lavatory pan.

I swung my feet to the carpet. The hotel was warm and dry, antiseptic. I switched on the TV set and got back into the middle of the film I'd watched the previous afternoon, then I took a bath.

Downstairs I ate breakfast alone in a corner of the restaurant; it was like eating in a mosque with your shoes on. The ceiling was high and I sat alone, confined in a superstitious quiet, where the waiters stood in groups, arms folded, exchanging unpleasant words about me in rough and foreign tongues. There was no point in fighting it and I never did. Instead, I thought of a certain Russian teaching which had flourished under the Czars. It taught silence and cunning, advising insignificance and selfishness as the only road to happiness; the individual had to go underground to preserve his individuality. I could never remember the name of the philosophy but every morning it became more and more reasonable.

I chewed and stared. Stretching across the far end of the room was the Morley table with its forty or fifty places. Since we'd arrived at the hotel, that table had never been completely vacated, there was always someone sitting there eating or drinking and there was now. Max sat at the head of it in a massive carver that looked like a throne. He too was chewing and gazing down the restaurant, looking deep into Billy's vacant chair.

Max had black hair, parted in the middle, falling in waves past little pink ears. The hair was carefully touched in with wise streaks of grey. He was portly and he bustled when he moved, like nothing was going to stop him, so get out of the way, you dummy. Young, genial, he was fired with that kind of ambition which is the most difficult to understand, the simple need to succeed at anything, something, no matter what. For all his geniality, Max's body looked powerful and his podgy hands were made for strangling; people he didn't like and people he did like as well if it suited him.

The Morley business had started by accident but was now the biggest of its kind in the world; and every time Max mentioned the fact, he glinted his teeth at you like a cat who'd cornered a cartoon mouse. There was nothing accidental about Max, he'd joined the company in its early days and he'd been with it ever since.

It had all begun in Connecticut, where Professor Morley had once occupied the chair of Biology in a small university, a position he'd soon been forced to relinquish, for, old-fashioned in his approach, he'd first been promoted sideways and then retired. During that forced retirement, the professor had taken up writing.

What he wrote was a series of quasi-religious articles about Nature, which were first published in the college quarterly and then, when there were enough of them, issued separately by the university press.

At first the fan letters arrived in small batches, but soon the professor found himself posting copies of his work to addresses all over his home state, and then eventually to states right across the continent. His retirement suddenly became more interesting than the whole of his previous career. "In the evening of my life," he informed his fellow academics, "achievement."

The professor had one daughter, Ruth, and she'd married, when quite young, a mail-order salesman with a pink face and a pointed skull, Freddie Beckenbauer, and the three of them lived in a white wooden house on the very edge of the campus. It was Freddie who persuaded the professor to collect his essays into a slim volume and to have them attractively bound and privately printed, and it was Freddie who circularised the professor's correspondents, telling them about the new book, which he called, *The Wisdom of Professor Morley: Nature's Way*. It went very well. Freddie reprinted and reprinted again.

Our life, said the professor, gained in intensity once we realised that there was a heart to nature, and that nature longed for us to find that heart. She wanted us to make our bodies clean, she wanted us to think straight and pure and then become what we thought. At the same time, Nature would help us to carve out our destinies with a new certainty because we had moved closer to her, we were nearer to her core.

It was a simple and refreshing philosophy and people could understand it. The professor wrote two more books and Freddie aimed mail-shots into a hundred thousand letterboxes, where eager hands caught them before they could hit the floor. Freddie resigned from his job and sat down to ponder the problem of realising the American dream in his own back yard. He could sense, from the letters the professor was receiving daily, that there was a hungry vacuum roaming the world looking for something to suck. What Freddie needed was a giant lollipop and he found it right under his hand, in the professor's own story.

As a youth, frequently unwell and often housebound, the professor had used all his spare time to research a project of his own, investigating the area where biochemistry met mysticism and magic. His quest had been to isolate a substance he called Life's Essence and, when he found it, which he did after five years of study, he made it into a powder and sprinkled the stuff onto everything he ate and, perhaps it was a coincidence, he became stronger. He had discovered nature's secret, a supplement that every food needed; better than vitamins, it was the Philosopher's Stone, ground down into an enchanted dust. He didn't know it but he'd struck it rich, like a witless prospector who camps in the dark and wakes to find that he'd slept on a nugget as big as his fist.

The professor had used the story of this discovery and its results as the basis of his first book, and almost all his correspondents had asked whether the Essence were available and, if so, to hell with the price.

Freddie and Ruth looked at each other across their kitchen table in Connecticut and understood. They cleared a room, installed a sink and a laboratory bench, hoisted the old man out of his armchair and encouraged him to produce the magic essence. They did a deal with a supplier of bio-degradable cartons, ordered labels and once again circularised every single person on their file. Professor Morley's Food Supplement hit the road and never looked back. It was the best thing since sarsaparilla, and it had religion.

Freddie's next move was to write the professor's fourth Book of Wisdom himself, using it to push the old man's thinking in the direction of profit. Spreading the Morley gospel was not only morally desirable, it also made good financial sense. Witness the word, sell the Supplement, make sure your family, your friends and your neighbours got into the good habit; welcome them to the hierarchy of unselfishness.

From the very beginning, Freddie intended to use the hierarchy as a sales' graph. Those whom you converted would, in time, branch out on their own, taking the Morley books with them; and right behind would come the whole range of Morley goods, because the Food Supplement, though fundamental, was not enough. The Essence could be incorporated into everything; a new natural detergent, toothpaste, floor

The Morley Way

polish, face cream, cornflakes. The more of Nature's goods you had in your home, the better person you were and the higher your status. Every Morley person was part of Nature's central mystery, and the more merchandise you shifted, why, then, the more people you had saved.

The main beauty of the system was that all orders filtered back to Freddie through a chain of command and everyone felt involved. The Great Chain of Wisdom, it was called, and each convert gained in self-esteem as the order papers went through his hands. As your sales improved, you moved up the ladder. You began as a Morley Instructor, you developed into a Morley Tutor. From Tutor you went to Mentor and, in the end, at a special area ceremony, you were created a Perceptor of the Great Morley Way of Wisdom, and in your control were hundreds of busy men and women. You supplied them with everything they needed and you earned a lot of money. It was pyramid selling but it was holy.

Freddie didn't go retail and he didn't bother himself with production either. He bought from established lines, added the Essence in his own warehouses, packed the product under the Morley label and then mailed it. It was perfect. Within two years, Ruth and he, and the professor, were millionaires. A little later, he moved his main office to New York and rented a skyscraper. A year later, he bought it.

It wasn't enough. Freddie knew that what America was swallowing Europe could swallow also. He would send over his best man; the operation would need money, care, expertise, hundreds of people. A new office would have to be established, local staff recruited, a publicity campaign got under way. That was how Max came to England, and within twenty-four hours of landing the Morley man had been pointed at Billy and Magic Lantern Road Shows.

"If you want to launch a new company," someone had said, "Billy Jay's the man you want. He's as mad as a bat, has the biggest ideas, will work himself to death, and he won't overcharge!"

I was doing a script at the studio when Max came to see

Billy for the first time, and I didn't like what I saw. When Max looked at you, it was like the Normans looking at Sussex. He seemed inoffensive enough at first, for he had one of those warm American smiles of sincerity that embrace you, bright and big; a wholesome smile lighting your way deep into the dark.

Max talked about the show and Billy hovered on the edge of combustion like an oil-fired domestic boiler. Max wanted something big and colourful; five screens, clever lighting, a set that would make the audience think of *Merrie Englande*, a suggestion of nature, mock moss, the wash of water on a continuous loop of sound. Atmosphere, dream music and the recorded words of the professor booming down every now and then as if from a clifftop. "The Moses Effect," Max called it. "I want lots of ciné inserts too. There'll be speeches, and inject some of your history," he said, "Hadrian's Wall, thatched cottages, duck ponds, beauty. . . ."

Billy loved that day. He strode about the studio, eyes blazing madder than ever, shaping the air with his hands, throwing new ideas across the room like party streamers. It was Billy at his best, enthusing over his own enthusiasm.

And Max liked what he saw. He switched on his smile and handed me the four volumes of Professor Morley to read. I looked as far into his eyes as I could. It was like looking through two buckets of sump oil, but I found something disturbing there nevertheless. Max believed in what he was doing and he wanted everyone else to believe it too. He knew all those books by rote, every Morley man did, everyone had to believe, everyone had to buy.

"They always call us corny," said Max, "until they look at the accounts."

Before he left, Max gave us the brief and told us he wanted a "feasibility study, soonest." Magic Lantern would have to present something like seven or eight shows over a four-week period. He wanted a huge set, impressive and tasteful. Nothing to be rushed, nothing to be late. The best crew, the best writers. The first show, and the last, would be aimed at an audience of journalists, national and provincial newspapers, television, radio. They were to get the best in wine, food, accommodation. The information they received would be sophisticated, they had to be made favourable to Morley, they had to see that it was not just a business, it was a way of life too.

As soon as the first show was over we were to take a simplified version on the road; up one side of the country and down the other. It would call for high-class planning. It would need a crew of about twenty; riggers to move the set through the night and an inner body of operators to handle the hardware that made the show run, Magic Lantern people. Max would follow along with his team of Morley men and women, a travelling office of experts, salesmen and philosophers.

Already the Morley Pioneers, Max called them that, had been in Britain for several months. They had contacted Church social clubs, Old Age Pensioner Associations, Women's Institutes. Thousands of people had been invited to the shows, Morley cells had been created to introduce the Food Supplement and it was going well. The Morley fervour had been transplanted in dripping chunks, like human hearts.

It was a great opportunity for Billy. If Max was satisfied with Magic Lantern there would be another three months taking the show around Europe. If Billy got his costings right he might just get rid of his overdraft this time. Max meant business, he was going to have the whole world living the Morley way, and the sooner the better. As for me, I would be stage-manager on three hundred pounds a week.

It was a marvellous day and Billy cackled as we stood at the window and watched Max climb into the huge black Cadillac he had brought with him from the States. Billy's studio was on the edge of Clapham Common and there were trees and grass as far as you could see. Four of Max's assistants, in dark suits identical to his, stood at the car doors and didn't get in until Max was sitting. It was like saying the last farewell to President Nixon and I looked up for the helicopter but there wasn't one. As the car moved away, Max pushed a hand through the gap at the top of his window and waved; it looked like a cow's udder, full and pink against the green of the field behind.

DAY 12

CHAPTER FIVE

The Reward

I was the first into the conference room that day of the show, and I was glad to be. There was an unusual smell of greenery; freshly-cut branches, spilled chlorophyll, something I couldn't place. At last, behind the set near the big doors, I discovered several piles of branches and a huge mound of creeper, lopped off at random. There was a heap of dark green leaves as well. They must have been cut before dawn because they were all wet with dew and the wounds were sticky with sap.

I picked up a branch and pulled a leaf from it. Jim came and stood beside me and looked at the forestry.

"What's all that for?" he asked.

When Jim spoke, foliage disappeared. He had a flat accent that reminded you of roundabouts and shops built in pale brick, and of draughty subterranean passages leading from one side of a dual carriageway to another, a place where drunks piss at night. His voice was an assurance that he came from a terrain where the underground stations bear threatening names like Hanger Lane and Perivale.

"For decoration," I answered, "and to make you think of Nature, and to cover the pillars and the exits, Billy's control panel, and yours. They don't want to see you."

Jim was twenty-three and claimed a deep knowledge of oral

sex. I never discovered whether his experience was real or imaginary, but I did know that he believed in it. It was his stories of strange encounters of the mouth that kept us awake on the mortorways. Jim was our antidote to everything.

He was thin and knock-kneed, and his face looked only six years old and was oddly flat, falling straight down from forehead to chin. Round the chin grew a luxurious beard and on the top lip a moustache. The beard was a gingery colour like the hair on his head, which he parted in the middle and combed down on each side over his ears. Everything he wore was made of blue denim, except his tan cowboy boots; they had high heels and he strode in them, lifting each foot with a strut as if each step he took was to kick a cat. When he walked, his eyes glittered. When he stood still, his tongue moistened his lips every second. He looked like a randy squirrel, peering through a hedge, ready to leap on the first female squirrel that went by.

"Owdjer think he got on last night?" he said.

"All right, I shouldn't wonder. You'd better get up there and check through your lights, Max will want a full technical run-through as soon as he gets here."

"Screw Max," said Jim, but he walked away, scuffing the carpet with his heels.

I went under the stage and flicked on the pump that pushed our moat over and under the set. The water began to move, splashing down the rocks in front of the church.

I came out from underneath and found Billy standing there. "Hi," he said, his voice hoarse with alcohol, and his eyes dimmed by guilt.

"I've checked the power circuits," I said, "do you want to do it again?"

"Yeah," he said. "How was Max?"

"Last night? He said your first loyalty was to him and his cheque book."

Billy made a gesture at the set. "Bunch of krauts," he said, "no flair, no history."

"Yeah," I said, "they understand money though, that's worth a lot of history, that is."

Billy ignored what I'd said and dragged me into a corner beneath the back-projection gantry. "Yesterday afternoon," he whispered, "incredible."

"I thought it might be."

"No, straight up."

I leant back against the scaffolding. I knew I was due for one of Billy's stories. He told me about the men in police uniforms and the trip down the motorway, the unloading at Waddestone and the ride to Oxford, and he told me about making love to Casey and what it was like. It was one of Billy's best stories; I opened my eyes as far as I could and tried to appear surprised. He expected us to believe him.

"I don't want you to tell the others," he said. "I mean, this kind of knowledge could be dangerous."

"Okay Billy," I said, and walked away to get on with my work.

I didn't believe Billy of course, except when he'd said about Casey, but I was shaken a moment later when Jim came down to borrow a pair of pliers and showed me the *Daily Express*. It had the full story of the robbery on the front page. The headlines alone took up half the tabloid:

ROBBERY. Heathrow gang strikes again. Several armed and desperate men, dressed as police officers, overpowered employees of the Armacor security company yesterday and made off with a huge haul in diamonds, Kruger-rands and platinum. In a well-planned and executed raid, it is feared that the raiders escaped with upwards of a million pounds worth of valuables. Detective Inspector Alex Fisher, of the newly-formed bullion squad and in charge of the case, admitted today that while investigating all avenues, he was hoping for members of the public to come forward. The insurance companies have offered a massive reward, and, depending on the exact value of the goods stolen, it could rise to a HUNDRED THOUSAND POUNDS, possibly more.

Jim was very excited by the money. "Look at that," he said. "Great, eh, great. Wish I had some of it."

I handed the newspaper back to Jim. "Have you shown this to Billy yet?"

"No," he said, "I haven't."

There was a movement at one of the doors and Max entered the room in a flurry of acolytes and stood still, only moving his face like a searchlight, identifying us one by one.

Max worked from the main Morley office which had taken over the top floor. Under his supervision, forty or fifty employees managed the Morley invasion; transport, hotel bookings, banquets, invitations, payments. Every one of them wore a bleeper and Max's special aides carried walkie-talkies as well. Without moving out of bed, Max could make the whole world sweat.

The special aides followed Max everywhere, fanned out to the rear like tiny barges in the wake of an ocean-going tug. That morning they jostled near him, six of them, smart in suits and light-coloured shirts. They had good healthy skins with plenty of food bulging inside. There was a glossy black and white photographic look to those men, two-dimensional and celluloid, but only the best. They loved Max, they had to, he could garotte their careers in a second: not one of them wanted to make a mistake.

Max advanced into the room and his men followed. Billy appeared stage-left, beckoned me to him and we began the long walk to the centre of the hall. Two against seven; the gun-fight at the OK Corral.

"Well Billy," said Max, "we missed you at the rehearsal." His voice was unbeatable, green-coloured coconut icing, poisoned.

"Hell, I'm sorry Max, I got called to Liverpool. I couldn't let them down. I knew the boys could manage."

Billy made his voice sound apologetic. I nodded and smiled humbly. Max's own smile switched on and off like a bishop's.

He carried a big black file in his crossed arms. He held it backwards, without looking, and one of his runners stepped forward to receive it. It was like the missal changing sides during mass. Max put his fat stranglers together, interlacing the fingers, and moved at Billy. Max could walk through people like they were ectoplasm, and that's how he walked through me then. He took Billy by the elbow and sat him down in one of the chairs, just as if Billy weighed nothing at all. Max sat by him.

I glanced at the aides and said, "Good morning," and they said, "Today's the day all right," but we were all listening to Max. He didn't say much.

"Billy, I am spending something like five million dollars to launch Morley in Europe. I am spending a million and a half in this country alone. Your little show is costing me somewhere around one hundred thousand pounds. You are making a lot of money out of me. You'll be making even more if I take you over to Europe. If that works out, you'll be on the way to becoming a very rich man. When I pay someone, Billy, I want them to be where I am all the time. If I bleep, I expect you to jump out of the wall; if I call you on the walkie-talkie, you come out of my ass. Is that clear?"

Billy flushed a deep red and bobbed his head like he was swallowing someone else's cold phlegm. It was the money that kept his mouth shut. He'd had a big cheque from Morley to get the show rolling but there was a lot more cash to come. All he said was, "The rehearsal was fine, Max, wasn't it? No problems?"

Max's hands appeared out of his shoulders, palms forward; benediction.

"No problems," he said, "except one." A finger came over his left shoulder and pointed. His aides shifted uneasily but the finger was for me. "I do not pay that dummy one hundred thousand pounds to run this show. I pay for you because I was told that you are the best in the country. If you let me down, Billy boy, I'll screw you into the ground head first and skin the soles of your feet."

Billy nodded. He looked at the set and wanted to throw Max over it—but didn't, still thinking of his overdraft.

Max held up his right hand, the sign of peace. "You're the best, Billy, and I want you here all the time, remember, we've got a show to do today."

He stood up and turned towards his men and they drew closer to him. "I want the banqueting manager in here, I want the bar staff, I want those chairs moved and the tables laid. I want to be ready for the meal at one, the show to roll at three."

Max's runners dispersed on their errands. He turned to look at me and said, "Go and find some work for Chrissake."

I twisted on my foot and went backstage and picked up my script, there wasn't anything else for me to do.

Max and Billy, the best of friends, went through a checklist together. Max, portly, contained by his suit. Billy, with his big body forcing its way past what he wore, orange shirt, blue trousers.

Though very different from each other, both men carried a conspicuous ambition about with them like a name-tag on a lapel. Billy's ambition was a barrel of unstable gunpowder, you might damp it down for a while but it could still explode without warning, launching him anywhere.

Max's desires had a different quality. They were clear and cold and he frightened with his certainty. He knew. Max believed in his own intelligence and believed that it had made the only true judgement of the situation in which he found himself. It followed that his actions were correct and, being correct, he might as well be efficient—and he was. Max was Freddie Beckenbauer's theology made flesh, a faith creeping forward, and Max knew it was the only way to travel. Billy's spirit lived from hand to mouth, he worked hard because he thought he might get somewhere. Max was already there waiting; Max was his own desire.

We rehearsed the show and then broke for lunch. The hotel was filling with the Morley guests, a thousand of them flown and driven in from all parts of the country, so Magic Lantern ate behind the set, on a long trestle table with no table cloth:

The Reward

electricians, riggers, drivers, and a lot of people I didn't know. Kevin I knew, it was his firm that supplied the riggers. He was a skinny curly-haired boy with a pale face, and the paleness, surrounded by the darkness of his hair, made him attractive. Billy had ordered the meal so it was large steaks and a trolley-load of wine standing by us. The show was only two hours away.

I sat with Billy on one side of me and Duncan on the other, and Duncan filled the glasses. I liked Duncan. He was short and bouncy, dark, he looked Jewish. Duncan had a natural genius when it came to machines, even Billy admitted that. Electricity was no mystery to Duncan; he knew where it went, by which route and at what speed. I never saw him lose his temper with machine or man, except Billy, of course, but if Jesus Christ himself had worked on one of Billy's shows there'd have been a fist-fight by the end of it.

I got the newspaper from Jim, folded it and put it over Billy's plate. We had all drunk wine that morning and Billy had difficulty reading at first and was forced to drop his head towards the print. Then his body straightened and in the same second his eyes burned themselves sober.

"A hundred thousand pounds," he said, "that would get me over the hump."

His voice rose sharply with the excitement. He sounded like Queenie saying, "My husband and I . . ."

"Over the hump," I said, "some hump . . . that kind of money would get you over Everest."

"That's about the size of my overdraft," said Billy, fingering the newspaper, "something in the Himalayan range."

Duncan leant over and took the newspaper. "Nice," he said.

Billy was staring at me. I could see that he had made up his mind.

"I know what I'd do," Duggie had the paper now, "if I knew where they were."

Billy snatched the paper out of Duggie's hands and stood

up. "I know where they are," he said. He looked down at me. "What would you do?"

"I don't know," I said, "it's a hypothetical question."

Billy leant forward and put his clenched fists on the table. "It's always hypothetical for you. If it wasn't for the work I throw your way you couldn't be so bloody hypothetical, could you?" He groped for his glass and got it to his mouth and drained it. "I'm going to phone Detective-Inspector Fisher," he said, and left us, striding to the edge of the set, in the direction of the nearest phone.

DAY 12

CHAPTER SIX

The Morley Show

I sat in the dark behind a table, a green-shaded lamp gave me enough light to follow the script. The noise of a thousand people eating, drinking and talking came from the other side of the set. It was the noise of a big animal. Tension from Duncan, Duggie, Billy and Jim, flowed down the long wires and into my headphones, into my brain.

Duggie's voice spoke into my ear, into everybody's ear. "How much longer, Billy?"

Billy's control panel was up on the balcony on the opposite side of the hall from Jim's; it was a mini computer made by him and his big hands. From where he stood, Billy could see everything that happened on stage and watch his tapes running through. He could talk to us all through the headsets and we could talk to him.

Right at the beginning of the show Billy would give the word for Duncan to press his button; the master tape would roll forward and its bleeps make the carousels turn and the slides drop. Once the show was in motion, it charged forward like a tank and it pulled us along behind. When the show ran, everybody ran, panting, heart bumping all the way. If a slide stuck, if a tape broke or a lamp failed it was repaired on the hoof by whoever was nearest.

"The coffee's going out now," said Billy, "the liqueurs are being left on the tables."

The voice of the banqueting manager came next; he had the spare headset at the back of the room, near the kitchens. "That's it gentlemen, we 'ave er-finish. It's-a all er-yours." He was Spanish.

We were silent for a while, until Jim began to sing softly to himself. It was his own version of the American hymn and he called it the Star Spangled Hampton, but he broke off after a while. "You should see this bit out here, third table in, what a pair."

"Shuddup," said Duggie.

"She's beautiful," Jim went on. "I'd like to sprinkle some of the old Food Supplement on her fanny, I can tell you."

We all laughed madly and the sound echoed round our headphones, then Max's voice carved its way in.

"You guys remember who's paying you and keep some respect going."

There was silence until Jim said, "He's lucky we can laugh at all."

Max didn't answer and we stopped talking. After a while Billy said, "The waiters are clearing coffee cups."

"Stand by and keep it cool," said Max, "I'm going backstage." He put his headphones down and a voice, Jim's, said, "Piss off, sailor."

"Take it easy," Billy said. "I'm going into the intro music, stand by, fans, Dunc . . . ready on house lights, Jim, Mike, Duggie. I'll cue you for Max's speech. Here we go. Thirty seconds, this is it. Okay, fellas, back on your heads!"

Billy pushed the introductory music high, it swelled, it was fat all over the room. Such music. It was nature, her power. There was Elgar, there was some "Merrie Englande," some "Jerusalem."

"Roll tape one," said Billy, "let's get these bastards creaming in their drawers."

He wound up the decibels and the hotel shook, right down to the lowest level of the garage. The Professor's voice came booming out of the speakers like the words of Isaiah from the pages of the Old Testament. Quotations culled from the First Book of Wisdom:

"I have searched and worked long years on this earth. Most of that time, and foolishly, I fought against Nature, against life. I swam against the tide until I saw the simplest thing, and I took Nature to my heart and wonder took me like a lover. I turned a simple turn and immersed myself in Nature's current, and struggled no more. Nature is our mother and our friend if we will but learn to speak to her. Nature will love us if we will love her."

We didn't use too much of the Professor's wisdom that day at Heathrow, we didn't dare with a critical audience. The presentation concentrated on the financial achievements of the company, the benefits that Morley had brought to its own people, the benefits it would bring to Britain. But the Professor had a good voice, deep and sincere, sodden with truth, and friendly; occasionally the script allowed it a moment of freedom and it rushed across the auditorium on its own.

"Food," said the voice, "is not enough. Nature has more. I have tapped Nature's hidden treasure and it flows through me, take what I offer. With men who believe in Nature, what can I not achieve . . . ?"

The tape carrying the Professor's words was pulsed directly into the lighting secreted around the room. As he spoke, so certain lights rose and fell, flashed and flickered and all our fresh greenery changed colour. Above me I could hear the projectors click and clatter, as the first of a thousand slides turned and fell in their carousels. Across our five screen sky great visions of nature appeared and disappeared, superimposed themselves on one another, faded away or were recalled.

Sounds rose. Elgar was gone and we sank into Mahler. Billy had cut the music about superbly, a skilful knife job by a top surgeon. It was all romantic, love remembered, and this was only the first five minutes.

I heard Billy speak, "We got 'em, we got 'em."

Another voice in the headset, this time muttering, Jim's.

"What a way to earn a crust, man, what a way to earn a crust."

I followed the script word for word, where it led me, through the past and into the future. In the gloom behind the set, I was surrounded by the performers; dancers, acrobats, speechmakers. In the darkness these people stood near me, waiting for me to touch them with my finger so that they could go on stage. If they were nervous I pushed them on. I had the band of a Scottish regiment too, ready to march and counter-march, swinging kilts and skirling bagpipes. Billy believed in military music and he was right. The audience loved it and beat their hands together and cheered.

About an hour into the show, Max came and stood beside me. He held his speech, rolled into a truncheon, and he was hitting his leg with it. Billy was still making the music run, pushing it hard and the Professor's voice rang out yearningly, as if trying to bring the music back. "But come with me and I will show you Nature's heart." I nodded at Max and he moved up the steps at the back of the set. I raised my finger as the big music disappeared in the distance; I dropped my finger and Max went on stage. When he was ready he spoke:

"We," he said, with his voice as round as a pumpkin, "have found the simple wisdom of Professor Morley a sure way into a better life. You," he paused, "are all men and women of the world, you have seen much and done much and yet you know in your heart of hearts that simplicity is wisdom. We have had to hustle, we have had to make a dollar, sure, but Professor Morley has shown us how to improve ourselves, our families, our friends. When we work we bring a spiritual richness to our daily dealings, and I want to show you not only how that is possible, but why it is necessary."

Max was taking them on; the best, the only way with such an audience. He did not speak at length, but with appropriate slides and film he explained what Morley was and what it meant to do. No one had understood at the beginning but he, Max, understood. Dedicated and serious men and women wanted to meet and work together. The Morley family spread its cells first across a county, then a state, then a nation . . . now a hemisphere. It was a web of steel, ordered but democratic; it had come to strengthen the fabric of our society, to protect us against the threat of totalitarianism by making the democratic process work. Morley taught us to be strong and self-reliant and yet to trust in our fellows. Above all, it taught us to work with Nature rather than against her; when we trusted her we trusted one another, when we trusted one another we were invincible, we were free.

While he spoke, Billy hosed the room with background music and Duncan pumped the slides in by hand, because Max had said that he might want to ad-lib. Onto the screen came pictures of the last congress in Mexico, maps of the Morley world, coloured graphs, Main Office, New York, factories bright and clean, portraits of the Professor staring into test-tubes, holding them up like binoculars, senile and smiling as he danced with Nature.

Max came to the end of his speech:

"I know that we are good, simply that, simply good. All our products are natural, they come from nature and are designed to return to her, as we are. But we are good for the people who work for us too, we take them into nature's heart, we give them pride, we give them reasons, we give them hope. We defend what is good but to survive we will have to remain strong. By the end of this century it is estimated that the entire commerce of the free world will be controlled by a mere hundred and fifty companies, multi-nationals. We in Morley are determined to be one of those companies," he paused and laughed, "if not two of them. We must be there, to protect our heritage and I'm going to make sure we are there. We've got to be."

Max went surfing out on a wave of Wagner and the show traipsed on. I had a crowd of young Americans round me now, and I checked their names against my list, getting them ready to go on stage. They were the witnesses of faith, they had been flown over to tell how they had joined Morley. As they went to the pulpit their photos appeared on the screens. Naive, warm faces, ten feet high and carved from cheddar with blackheads as big as bullet holes. As each one of them appeared before the audience, Billy bunged in a fanfare, while Jim gave them a spotlight and cheered into our headphones.

The last witness came off and a choir rose at the back of the balcony, bathed in a golden light, and sang the Morley hymns. When the music had faded away the voice of the Professor bounded in again and spoke to us of Europe:

"Europe and America need to touch, not through politicians, that has always failed, but on the level of the ordinary man; on the level of simplicity and wisdom. Morley can bind us together, separate but whole. With this new way comes a new comradeship, a new network to give national and international cohesion, a giant turnover that springs not from greed, competition and hatred, but from love. Out of the pure comes strength, out of Nature comes civilization."

And the music poured over everything, horn and drum and strings, rising up over the balcony. And then the great bank of light back-stage came alive as Jim slowly brought up the Dawn. The Morley sunrise grew and spread over the five screens; five slides went running across, one into the other, and there was Britain waking from sleep. The lights blazed from behind and coloured the sky and everything shone. Billy had said it would be great and it was, even from the back where I sat, incandescent in stage light, the sweat stiff on my shirt. The music was painful and still Billy gave it more; nobody could handle music like he could.

"They're standing up," Billy screamed down the wire, "what a show, they're standing up."

"Idiots," said Jim's voice, faint though he too was shouting.

"We've got 'em," said Billy, still screaming, "what a knock-out." His voice ran on, "Thanks, fellas, wonderful. Thanks, fellas. Thanks, fans, wonderful, wonderful. I've got a bottle of malt whisky up here, what am I saying, two bottles. Give them the houselights, Jim, slowly but right up."

"Slowly, but right up."

"Right up . . . then get round here, fellas, and, we'll have a drink; am I going to get smashed tonight? Right up, Jim."

DAY 12

CHAPTER SEVEN

Casey Leaves

We stood in an excited cluster of twenty or thirty people on the balcony near Billy and looked down at the audience gathering in clusters themselves. We drank the whisky.

During the show the Morley Pioneers had stood in the dark at the edges of the room; now, with the houselights up they moved among the guests, distributing presentation packs of Morley goods. Pretty girls came from all sides too, carrying brochures and lapel badges.

A wine waiter appeared at the far end of the balcony, pushing a loaded drinks trolley towards us; magnums of Dom Perignon, what Duncan called Jewish champagne. Billy watched it roll right up to him. "It's from old alligator teeth, bring glasses," he said, and waved his right hand in the air for service. But another waiter was already placing glasses on a trestle table that stood against the wall. Billy got the first glass and emptied it in a throw, half into his mouth and half into the open neck of his shirt.

Max pushed through a set of swing doors and bustled through the straggling crowd. He was holding hands with a woman who must have been his wife. She was dressed in pale clothes and her hair was black touched with grey, like Max's only longer. Apart from that, she might have been his reflection in a hotel mirror, his shadow on the carpet. Max's six runners followed the couple, smiling, proud to be there.

Max shook hands with us all, even with Kevin and the riggers. "Great work, fellas," he kept saying, "great work, it really was." He smiled, more warmly than usual. "Keep it up, now my work begins, I've got to go and talk to just about evrybody."

He walked away and we held our glasses high and laughed. I looked around me into a frieze of shining faces, faces that burned with wine. Under each raised arm every shirt was rotting with rings of salt, but it didn't matter. The first show was over and it was too early to think of the next, forty-eight hours away in Nottingham.

Billy sat and leant his head against the wall and grinned. Casey Roberts walked through the bunch of people I was standing with, took Billy's glass and drained it.

"Well," she said, "it all worked."

Billy nodded in agreement and drank his champagne from a bottle. He wagged a finger at her.

"I'm going to be rich, Casey, and it's all down to you, I won't have to do much more of this."

Casey didn't understand what Billy meant so I fetched the newspaper from the top of the control panel and she read the article. She was dressed in an outfit of powder blue, and had dark suede boots to the knee. The skirt she wore had pockets and one hand was thrust down as far as it would go, the other held the newspaper. She looked up.

"You've told the police?"

Billy's wine flush blazed warmer in his cheeks. "Fisher is coming," he said, "the goose is getting fat. What's it to you?"

"Nothing," she said, though she looked very angry. "I just don't like people who change their minds for money, that's all. Twopence, no; threepence yes."

"It's not threepence, is it? Do you want half?"

Casey's voice hardened. "I don't need money that much," she said. "I don't need it at all."

Then it was Billy's turn to be angry. He lurched in his chair

Casey Leaves

and grabbed Casey by the wrist, hurting her. He stretched his other arm at me, to point. "You're like him," he said, his face showing how much he had drunk during the day, "hypothetical, only he can't afford it and neither can I. Hypothetical is a luxury for you and people like you."

I filled Billy's glass. His head swung. "Casey," he said, "you and me are the same, only I eat money and you eat men." And it was there that Billy pulled her hand down and she walked away, and I fell into a chair and watched her disappear.

Billy didn't watch but raised his glass and gave us the toast. "Here's to money, boys, let money take the strain. Whatever the pleasure, money completes it. Money is good for you . . . you're never alone with a wad."

Billy's eyes went opaque and out of focus and he smiled, like cheese melting slowly in the sun. He wasn't seeing any more. His shoulders lowered, the big arms pushed the glasses away and, into the clear space on the table, he dropped his large and untidy head, asleep.

As soon as his head went down I left the conference room; I wanted to see Casey, wanted to say something.

I was strangely aware of the colours of the hotel, they had become brighter, yet were soft-edged and hazy. I walked through reception, holding onto the long desk where the girls in fawn uniforms sat. They looked at me. There were clumps of people all over the hotel, drinking, sitting in corners, opening their mouths wide to laugh. Max's guests held shiny portfolios of publicity and golden sachets of Food Supplement. Banners covered the walls, reading TRY THE MORLEY WAY.

I wandered up and down the ground floor, not minding the looks I got as I stumbled between, and sometimes through people, looking into their faces, looking for Casey.

I got to the entrance foyer and the porters stared. I was in a huge and wasteful area where an amber gleam fell from down-lights in a ridged ceiling, and the glare was thrown up into the eyes by huge paving stones of polished black plastic.

Square slabs of amber-tinted upholstery littered the place; people were sitting on them and they looked at me. Everything was amber, the doors that led from the foyer to the outside, they were plate glass, fully automatic and amber-coloured too.

I glanced out to measure the daylight, hoping to discover what time it was. I didn't manage it but there was someone out there I knew. I glanced down at my watch and it told me the time, the day, the month and the year.

It was Casey who stood outside under the concrete awning, waiting for a taxi, her back towards me, unmoving. I took my time and made myself stand up straight.

Casey's right foot was stuck out sideways from her body, balanced on the heel of her boot. She was composed and relaxed, she knew exactly where she was, exactly what she was doing. She looked separate from everything else, and yet there was a deep carnality in her that showed through her skin. She made me feel gauche and inadequate.

I felt dirty from the work, from the show. I glanced at my hands, they were filthy, oily, I hadn't washed to eat. My hair itched. I hesitated, her taxi hadn't come. I wanted to speak to her before she left, I just wanted to. My breath smelt and I was drunk but I went out, raising my hands to the doors that opened on their own.

The daylight was a shock. I couldn't remember when I'd last been in it, it made me feel cold even though it was August. I stood behind her and, keeping my voice as tight to my thoughts as I could, I said, "I hope Billy didn't annoy you." It was pathetic, but I wanted the words to get to her brain before she knew who had said them.

I got what I deserved. She turned and I could see her mind spinning free, fast, like a lathe, then she realised who I was and I saw her ease right down to engage the correct gear, the slowest. I smiled and shivered. There was a bright greyness of light falling from cloud, like soot. She looked at me through grit and the wind played with a sheet of old newspaper it had brought up from the motorway.

Casey Leaves

"Why did you go off with him in the van?" I had to be stoned to ask that.

Casey gave me one of those upper-class charity smiles, like the lady of the house discovering that the daily help reads the *Spectator*.

"You mean with him, rather than with you?" Her glance took me in, rinsed me clean and threw me out, all in a second, like a machine dealing with the weekly wash. "For fun," she said, "just for the hell of it."

Her taxi turned the last curve in the road and came towards us. She picked up her hold-all, dark leather, expensive, like her clothes. The words "over-privileged cow" went through my mind, but they didn't exorcise her for me.

The taxi drew up and a little gnome poked his head out of the window.

"Bugger him," I thought. I staggered once more as, seconds late, I moved to help Casey with her bag. "Look," I said, "where are you going now?"

"I have to go to Brussels for a while," she said. She shook her hair on purpose. I lowered my gaze; why the hell should she get away with it?

"It's only a body," I said. "It's only the luck of the draw."

"You're out of your depth," she answered, and she got into the cab, leaving the door open for me to slam.

The taxi spun in a tight circle and the driver grinned up over the dashboard, his hands furry on the steering wheel. As he drove away he leered, and it was a leer that had motored through decades of adultery and fornication. He was an expert that driver, often hired to carry excuses and flowers in his empty cab from one lover to another.

I watched the black taxi disappear down towards the motorway. "You bitch," I said, "you bitch." Casey didn't hear me and it wouldn't have mattered if she had. Uncertain on my feet, I turned and went back into the amber hotel.

DAY 12

CHAPTER EIGHT

Detective-Inspector Fisher

I went straight to the conference room and, when I got there, I found that Kevin and his riggers had already begun to strike the set. The moat was leaning in sections against the stage, the pulpit was down and so was half the church. On the balcony, Jim was dismantling the lighting board and unplugging cables. Duncan and Duggie were passing projectors from the rostrum to the floor and packing them into wooden cases. My job was to get the carousels together and stack them away in order, making sure they were correctly labelled.

After an hour or so Billy joined us, he was puffy-eyed and his head looked loose on his neck. He had a litre of chilled white wine with him and he took it to the balcony and began to strip down his control panel, stacking the tapes away with heavy hands, drinking now and then.

I was leaning on the balcony rail, taking a drink from Billy's second bottle, when the police arrived. Only two of them came as far as us, though I could sense that there were a lot of them in the hotel. Our two weren't in uniform.

"Fisher," said one, "Detective-Inspector Alex Fisher."

He showed us a card which meant nothing and we nodded as though it did.

"Are you William Jay?" The tone he used made the name sound criminal, like he'd really said, "Are you Dr. Crippen?"

Billy grinned and said that he was and sat down on his swivel chair. There were other chairs nearby and I sat down on one. The policemen stood.

"You said on the phone that you had some information . . ."

Billy waved his bottle, offering a drink, and the policemen shook their heads; they looked impatient with him already. Billy shrugged and said, "Do you have any idea where they went, who they were?"

"We're following normal lines of enquiry, this is just one. We'll get them sooner or later."

Billy gave his maddest cackle and spun his chair round two full turns and swigged on the move from his bottle. "Like the five or six other Heathrow robberies," he said, when he'd stopped spinning.

Fisher looked at me but I didn't say anything or do anything.

Billy lurched upwards from his chair and his heavy torso and belly surged at the police officer.

"I can tell you where they are, and where all the money is, and I know how long they're going to be there." Billy gestured with the bottle, and a slurp of silver wine curved like a fish between me and the electric light before disappearing into the carpet.

"I got a van down there," Billy said, and the policeman turned and watched as Jim backed Panurge into the room and parked it alongside the pantechnicon. "That front bit, the luton, is a bedroom. I was sleeping in it when those guys nicked it to move the stuff. I was with them all the way." Fisher's assistant stared at the riggers as they slid the stage flats into their lorry.

"You found the cars yet?" Fisher shook his head, letting Billy talk. "Course you haven't. I know where they are." Billy held back, Fisher waited. "They're on the bottom level of this garage here, covered in plastic sheets. You'll probably find that the man who runs the garage was straightened so as not to find the cars too soon." Billy up-ended his bottle and some liquid went down his shirt.

Fisher's number two leant over the balcony and called out. I got to my feet and looked over the rail. Two uniformed men were standing there, watching the riggers with a rough and ready animosity. There was a strong smell of pot floating up to us and, looking down, I could see fine pools of hazy-blue smoke lying here and there between me and the conference-room floor.

"I wasn't sleeping in the luton," said Billy, "but the lady is neither here nor there. It's got a window in the front, we went all down the M4, through the village, past the church and the telephone-box at the end of the street; a big house in its own grounds."

"How many men?"

"Five." Billy sat down.

"What makes you think they'll still be there?"

"I heard enough, when they were unloading, they aren't going anywhere for a couple of days, see what you lads do. When they move they'll go straight out of the country, Heathrow Airport and back home."

"Could you recognise them?"

"One of them, sure; the others, hardly."

Fisher stopped listening. He leant forward from the rail, uncrossed his arms and put his index finger in front of Billy's eye as if he were going to push it in and scratch the skull from the inside. "All right," he said, "if you are giving me the runaround, Fatty, I'll come straight back here and slim you down." The threat came quietly from a man who knew about physical violence, and it had all the power of the police force behind it. Billy was too drunk to notice.

"The reward's for the recovery of the property, that's all I want. I wouldn't contact you fairies for light conversation, would I? Take a good look at me, Fisher, I wouldn't want you to give the money to the wrong fella."

Fisher took a good look at Billy and I was glad he wasn't taking it at me. "The name of the village?"

Billy hesitated, looked at me. "You witness this, Mike." Fisher smiled, I nodded and Billy said, "Waddestone. Exit thirteen on the M4, travelling west. Do you want my employees to round them up for you?" Billy always said "my employees" when he was putting on the style.

The policemen exchanged glances of exasperation and turned to go. Just then, one of the uniformed men shouted from the opposite balcony. "They've found the cars!"

Fisher flicked his chin to his right shoulder and gave Billy a look of hatred, then he ran for the stairs, his assistant following. Billy span round in his chair, totally happy, his feet lifted from the floor. He laughed loud so the policemen could hear him as they ran. "Be careful, Fisher, they've got guns!"

I snatched Billy's bottle from him. If the cars were in the Stardust garage then the story was true, all of it. I had heard so many untruths from Billy, each one petering out into nothing, that I only ever listened to him on a wavelength of disbelief. Now here was a true story, the first, and I wondered what would come out of it. I stared at Billy, but he only laughed at me and snatched the bottle back and gurgled wine into his throat.

As soon as the pantechnicon and the van were loaded we ate a meal in the hotel's coffee shop, open twenty-four hours a day. Billy left us early, driving the Volvo, in a hurry. "I drive better pissed," he said, "like I work better pissed. Anyone want to come along for the quick ride?" He always looked hurt when we refused, but it didn't matter to us and there were no takers. He took the lift down to the garage, another bottle under his arm. I think Billy had stolen a magic bottle from out of a fairy story; it never emptied and it appeared whenever he rasied a hand above his shoulder.

I drove Panurge to begin with, Jim and Duncan sat beside me on the bench seat, Duggie took a turn in the luton. He spoke to us once on the mike, before he went to sleep. "It stinks of woman up here," he said.

Fully loaded, Panurge wouldn't do more than forty-five

miles an hour. It wasn't far to Nottingham but it took us three hours. The others slept while I tried to stay awake. Those trips at night were like driving round and round the hotel car park; at the end of it all was another hotel and another conference room, identical to the ones we'd left. Lights up, lights down, hour after hour. Panurge ground on, following the oil-droppings across the concrete flags.

Half way to Nottingham, Jim took the wheel and I tried to sleep. I couldn't, mainly because Jim kept talking about Eunice, Billy's regular mistress. She was the reason why Billy had been in such a hurry. Eunice, flown up from London, was at the next hotel, waiting soft and warm in bed, like a half-filled hot-water-bottle.

"I wish I had her on the end of mine," said Jim, putting his knees together even though he was driving. "I'd wave her about like a banner."

It was two in the morning when Duncan brought the truck off the motorway and up to the Hotel Sayonara. We went immediately to the conference room and checked it over. It was custom-built; long enough, wide enough, high enough and with enough power. We watched the riggers for five minutes, they were already unloading. "Oh, shit," I said, "let's do our bit in the morning."

In the deserted reception area we found a machine and each got a can of beer from it. We sat for a while on S-shaped sofas of yellow, drank from the sharp-edged tins and burped and blinked at each other. We were in the same place, different colours but the steel doors of the lifts were working away on their own. It was the American thing, planned right down to the last detail.

"I reckon," said Duggie, "that they get this bloody hotel on wheels and shove it up the motorway in front of us. I wonder who tells them where we're going?"

"Yeah," said Jim.

We finished our beers and stood up, rattling our room keys. "Let's go to bed," I said, "we've got Max tomorrow."

We trooped into an open lift and it closed its doors behind us.

We stood there, waiting to be raised. All our journeys were the same.

DAY 13

CHAPTER NINE

The Man from the Mirror

In the morning I opened my eyes, looked at my watch and found myself in the same old bedroom, just as tidy. You couldn't win against the hotel chambermaids. No matter how carelessly you threw your clothes down, no matter how many pens or ashtrays you stole, they had you beat. As soon as your back was turned someone grew out of the carpet, like a toadstool, and replaced everything, made the bed and disappeared without trace. In the bathroom, the underneath of the soap wasn't damp and there was a band of paper over the lavatory pan telling you that it had been sterilised—from what, it didn't say.

The phone rang and Duggie said, "We're in Billy's room, making coffee. She's here. Billy wants you come up, or is it down or sideways." Then, without warning, he put the phone down.

Duggie was like that, small and abrasive, a countenance you could strike safety-matches on, half the size of anyone else and twice the trouble. He always looked aggressive, like a prize fighter ready to take on all-comers because his real opponent had run away. When people reacted to Duggie's attitude he was quite prepared to hit them—and I'd seen him do it, hard. He'd taken one of his dislikes to me years before but, as we worked together fairly frequently, we had managed to restrict the antipathy and it only showed now in the silences.

I didn't go straight to Billy but took the lift to a corner of the conference hall. The riggers and the pantechnicon had gone during the night, the room was quiet, just how I liked it. I walked across the carpet and inspected the set. It was all together, not a seam showing; the moat, the screen, the church, the cottage. I went back to the lift and pressed a button. It was part of my job to keep Billy informed.

I wandered about the corridors for a while before I found his room, 5085. They never tried to do anything with the corridors; just drink machines, and red telephones in case of fire. Billy's room was easy to recognise because the door was off the hinges and leaning against the wall. Billy was the only man I knew who could make those hotels human.

He'd arrived feeling pretty hungry the night before and had phoned up to the room for Eunice to join him in the restaurant, and there they had eaten an enormous and expensive meal and drunk a great deal of burgundy. Back upstairs they discovered that Eunice had left the key locked in the room. Reception weren't much help, they kept saying that the porter would see to it, but the porter was doing something else and the chambermaids had long since gone home. As Billy got angrier, the hotel staff closed ranks and combined against him. Billy threatened them with adverse publicity, told them how much money he and Morley were going to spend in the place and asked for a manager. Nothing worked. In the end Billy went down to the Volvo for his tool-box, took it upstairs and removed the door. When the manager did arrive, with two porters and a security man, Billy and Eunice were in bed, drinking gin and watching television. The manager had wanted to throw Billy out of the hotel but had been reminded that Billy could hold up payment of a very large account, many thousands of pounds. "Goodnight," Billy had said with his hand on Eunice's crutch. "Move the door over on your way out."

I leant the door against the door-frame and stepped past it and into Billy's room. It was the *levée du roi*. Duncan was placidly making coffee for us all, like a self-satisfied housewife. Duggie was staring at the television set and Jim, flat-faced and expressionless, was watching every movement made by Eunice's bosom as she sat in bed, only half-covered by a pink bedjacket of brushed nylon. "They're like little piglets in candyfloss," he said to me, wonder in his voice. It was seven o'clock in the morning.

"What's going on downstairs?" Billy asked, using his big voice.

"It's okay," I said. "The set's up, we can shove our bit in as soon as we like and we can do a technical lunchtime."

Billy touched Eunice under the bedclothes and Jim tightened his lips. Eunice smiled and arched her throat.

Eunice was blonde, like Casey, but her hair was longer. Billy went for blondes, though Fran, his wife, was a brunette. Eunice had a very pretty face; pretty was the word, so was empty. She had wide cheekbones and a turned-up nose and big blue eyes. She looked sweet and wholesome, she was the girl next door and did a lot of advertising work because of it. Her features were perfect and she thought the rest of her was too; she never made the slightest effort in any direction. She flowed along, like our mechanical moat, round and round.

Billy had met her a couple of years previously while producing a floor-polish commercial in a studio in Dean Street. In no time at all he had convinced Eunice that he was going places in films and that she, if she wished, could go with him. He hadn't launched her yet but she didn't mind the waiting. Billy splashed money all over her like it was deodorant and treated her as if she were already a star. She ate well, dressed well and flew all over the world to meet Billy whenever he had five minutes to spare. They'd holidayed in the Bahamas, gone touring in Japan, filmed in Morocco. She hardly spoke and never expressed an opinion. Jim fancied her with all his slim body, so beautiful she was, more than anything he had ever got his hands onto or his teeth into. She was straight off the television screen. Everyone looked at her when she passed, and Billy loved her. Duggie said that being with Eunice was like looking through an old colour supplement, waiting at the dentist's; it was lightweight, chocolate-box and frightening all at the same time.

Billy got out of bed and walked to the bathroom, naked; Eunice yawned, not a sound passed the double glazing from the motorway outside. Billy's body was too white and his stomach and his buttocks wobbled when he walked. Even his large head looked small on top of so much flesh.

There was a knock at the door which was still leaning at an odd angle. It slid and fell over. I went to the doorway and found a red-faced man picking the door up. He was wearing a light summer overcoat but no hat, he was about forty years old, nearly bald and with a map on his face that showed many years of drinking. I could tell he had just come into the hotel because there was fresh air sticking to the weave of his coat.

"Yes?"

"The workmanship in these hotels is terrible," he said, and propped the door against the corridor wall. "Billy Jay in?"

"He's in the bath, what do you want?"

"I'm a friend of his, J. S. Kelly, *Daily Mirror*."

I wasn't going to let him in just like that, especially a newspaper man. "Have you got any identification?" I asked him. "We get a lot of funny people up here."

Kelly looked at the dismantled door. "I'm not surprised," he said, "perhaps you are a lot of funny people up here." He showed me a card which said "John Stephen Kelly, *Daily Mirror*." I handed it back and nodded.

He smiled and said, "They don't mean a lot, I've got another one that says I'm Princess Anne."

"You couldn't be," I said, "your manners are too good."

The sound of Billy's voice came from the bathroom. "Oh, let him in, come on, Kelly." I stepped aside and Kelly passed into the room, a photographer appeared from the corridor and followed him.

Kelly went directly into the bathroom; the photographer sat in an armchair and studied Eunice. Duncan, Duggie and

Jim left to make a start on the show. I went to follow but an order from Billy stopped me; gin and tonics all round, lots of ice.

I got everything I needed from the machines and gave Eunice and the photographer a large drink each. They hadn't opened a conversation; Eunice was probably unaware that the population of the room had changed. I took the other drinks into the bathroom, Kelly was sitting on the closed lid of the WC, looking at the folds of Billy's flesh, squeezed like marshmallow into the beige bath-tub.

I first gave Billy his pint of gin and tonic and then Kelly. The reporter looked at his drink, impressed in spite of himself. I had a glass too, and, without being invited, I sat on the bidet to listen.

". . . Anyway," Kelly was saying, "they picked them up last night, and all the stuff, Kruger rands, diamonds, bits and pieces. I was at the police-station when they brought them in, thanks for the phone call; by the way, they were Americans."

"Their accents were."

"They must have flown over just to do the work, they didn't say a thing, didn't look put out. Real professionals."

Billy rubbed lather under his armpits. "Can you do me a piece?"

"If there's nothing else on I could even make the front page with it. It's a good story, big reward, ordinary man beats international bullion gang, especially that bit about the luton."

"You can't use that," said Billy.

"Pity," said Kelly, "what will you do if you get the reward?"

Billy waved a hand and threw water over Kelly's trousers. "Take a long holiday from this business. Go into films, produce my own, good quality stuff."

Kelly nodded. "You should get quite a chunk of money, all that's going, anyway. Without your say-so they'd never have got near those four guys."

Billy sat upright in the water. "Four," he said, "there were five of them. Bloke with greasy blond hair, cut short. Old-fashioned-looking bloke. Brylcreemy, moustache, square face, hard mouth."

Kelly shook his head. "Only four found in the house at Waddestone, only four brought into the police-station, plus the loot."

"Well, I'm buggered," said Billy. "I wonder where the other one is?"

"I hope he's not vindictive," I said, "for your sake."

"Yes," said Kelly, "he's got an awful lot to lose his temper about. Look, if you got dressed we could take a couple of pictures."

I stood my empty glass in the sink. "I'm going downstairs," I said.

As I left, Billy called, "Leave the keys to the truck, I want to show Kelly the luton."

DAY 14

CHAPTER TEN

Mr. Nasty

Past midnight, that night. Billy, Eunice and I were sitting in the coffee shop. Billy had his head in his hands, quiet, almost asleep. All the others had gone to bed, exhausted, Morley men as well. Eunice had been resting all day and looked fresh and lovely. She was eating zabaglione and turning over the pages of *Cosmopolitan*. I was half asleep myself, drinking my way down some red wine and making sure that Billy's glass always had something in it. The coffee shop was deserted; two night-shift waitresses sat at a table about a hundred yards away and talked.

We had rehearsed all afternoon and all evening, working until Max had been satisfied, changing the show because the audience was changing. From now on our message was a simple one—less razzamatazz but with the hard sell hardened, talking directly to the people chosen by the Morley Pioneers to sell the Morley products door to door across Britain. It was our job, over the next couple of weeks, to energize the earnest punters, inspiring the husband and wife teams with wisdom, faith and the hope of honest reward. Every time we ran the show, Max said, there would be more than a thousand Morley recruits watching it.

A big man that neither I nor Billy had ever seen before came and sat down at our table and began talking to us like he was an old friend. I wasn't surprised. There were a lot of lonely people in those hotels and late at night was their time.

The man smiled. "I'm from Vauxhall Insurance," he said. "I'd like a word with you."

Billy didn't even raise his head. He left the polite chit-chat to me.

I said, "That's nice, would you like a glass of wine?" The man looked at the label on the bottle and shook his head.

There was not much to like about the man's face, it didn't have an amiable line on it anywhere. It was shiny and clean and the ears had fleshy lobes. The man was fat all over and his skin was tight; he looked like a flesh-coloured balloon filled with warm water, but he was all muscle. There was a lightness of movement to him that made him sinister. His eyes were as thin as razor-blades; yellow, and the eyebrows ran into one another, straight and patchy like old emery-boards. His suit was navy blue, worn shiny at the elbows and cuffs, but neither the cloth nor the cut was cheap; it was just that he did a great deal of office work. There was an abundance of power in him and patience too, and the patience was part of the power. Inside this fat man there was no thin man trying to get out, there was just another fat man. I looked at him as he read the label on our wine and I thought how nasty he looked. And that's what I called him, Nasty.

"Vauxhall Insurance," I said, "yes, that's nice." Eunice didn't look up from her zabaglione.

"Your life insured?" asked Nasty.

"Mine isn't," I said. "Billy's is, for thousands."

"You ought to be insured, you should think of your dependents."

"I haven't got any."

"The young lady, then, is she insured? Beautiful like that, she should insure her face, her body." Nasty could make the word "body" sound like the title of a pornographic magazine. This made Eunice look up and she smiled like a damp flannel and looked down again. Billy still didn't raise his head. I glanced to my left and, beyond a row of potted plants, saw four men sitting on a yellow settee in reception. They wore dark suits and ties, awkwardly, like they'd just swung down from the trees to try them on. They looked wrong for the hotel but they looked right for Nasty. I could feel their rough hands on my body, doing what they liked, and I smiled at Nasty and decided to be polite.

"I think you're right," I said, "we don't take insurance seriously enough. I often think it ought to be compulsory." With those four apes following him around, Nasty could have made homosexuality compulsory.

"I have had a lot of experience in the insurance business," he said, "and I want you to tell your friend, when he wakes up, not to become too excited about this reward. You know it all comes through insurance companies and they can take an awful long time. Indeed, when the reward does come, it is never as easy as you imagine or as large as you deserve."

"I don't believe it, anyway."

"You are very wise," said Nasty. He seemed delighted.

Billy raised his head. He looked terrible, half asleep, drunk, and hair all over the place. "What business is it of yours?" he said, "Piss off, Fatty."

I made urgent signs at Billy with my eyes and head, trying to tell him about the four men in the reception, but he, true to his nature, thought I was nodding encouragement.

"It's my business, all right," said Nasty, pleasantly, turning his face to Billy, "though all I really wanted to do, simply, was to point out, as a friend, that where a huge amount of money is involved, as in this case, one must not expect all of it to arrive in one's personal bank account, that would be unreasonable. Where large sums are at stake there is always competition."

Billy sat up, blood rushed to the crow's feet in the angles of his eyes and the anger made him younger, but there was no humour in his face, he'd woken in the worst of moods.

"Who the hell do you think you are? If it hadn't been for me the law would have got nowhere, it's all down to me, all of it."

Nasty tapped his fingers on the tablecloth, playing with his patience like a man playing with the lid of a boiling kettle, letting us see just how hot it was inside.

"That's as may be," he said. "I am just saying, still as a friend, that it doesn't do for a man to build his dreams too high, things never turn out as we wish, it's common sense, Billy."

I felt frightened. Billy didn't like strangers calling him Billy, he didn't like being bullied or taken for a ride, especially in front of witnesses, especially in front of Eunice. I eased my chair back a bit. I knew how Billy worked; violent in a moment.

"I have enough friends to call me Billy," he said. "I have accountants to tell me how far I can dream and more than enough insurance. I'm a rich man, dead. Why don't you go screw yourself?"

I winced. It was no good looking at Eunice, she hadn't heard a word.

Nasty gave a little half-shrug of the muscles in his shoulders and stood up. "Very well, Billy, but you will have to talk to me again, one day. I hope your tour goes well, A-V shows must be a worry, so susceptible to human error, aren't they?" Nasty smiled and put his chair tidily against the table.

There was nothing that made Billy angrier than a threat to his show. All Billy's being went into his material, menace or criticise it and you kicked him where it hurt most. In a second he had lost his temper; he rose and seized Nasty by the collar and the trousers. Nasty was a very heavy man but all Billy's strength came when he called it. He got Nasty off the floor and threw him onto a table, laid for breakfast.

Nasty might have been trained in office work but he had been trained in something else too. He rolled with the throw and allowed himself to slide along the cloth, sweeping all the cutlery and dishes with him. He came neatly off at the table's end and took gently to the floor on his toes, straightening his lapels with both hands, almost before he had stopped moving. His control was uncanny and scared me sick.

Beyond Billy the four men had stood up and were half way towards us, their knuckles knocking on the floor, but Nasty stopped them, raising a hand. He wasn't hurt, he wasn't ruffled. Billy at last saw the men and tried to look like he didn't care and swallowed hard. The two waitresses at the far end of the room stood up and moved a couple of steps towards us but then stopped and looked round for someone to come and help them. Nobody came and they sat down to watch. Billy picked up a bottle from the table and backed against the nearest wall, indicating that I should pick up a bottle too. I didn't and got ready to run instead, choosing a route into the kitchens. Eunice didn't move.

My cowardice was not necessary. Nasty turned and left the restaurant, his men followed. A head waiter came in and shouted at the girls in Spanish, looked at Billy, saw the bottle in his hand and then went away. I sat down, trembling, and drank some wine.

Billy came and stood at the end of the table and poured himself a glass too. Eunice stroked his hand with her own. "Who the Saint Fairy-Anne was that?" Billy said.

"Some friends of the guys you put inside," I said, "who else?"

"Well, what was all that Mother Hubbard about insurance for?"

"I dunno, but whatever they said, what they meant was clear, they want some of your money."

"Well, they're not getting it," said Billy, pulling Eunice to her feet, "I want it."

I lagged behind the other two as we crossed reception and half way to the lifts a man stopped me. He came up from a yellow armchair and took me by the elbow with his thumb and forefinger. We stood together watching, as Billy and Eunice were shut in by a pair of lift doors. Just before he disappeared, Billy touched his watch to indicate that I should get to bed. His eyes slid over the man next to me and I could see that Billy didn't appear to recognise him. I changed my weight from one foot to another. I don't like strangers touching me, though I was not prepared to do anything about it—not after the scene in the coffee shop.

With the change in stance, my elbow came away from the man's grip. I half-smiled to make up for it, and looked into the man's face; it was a flat face on a bullet head. His hair was cut close to the side of his skull though it was long on top; it had been blond but was now made dark by thick haircream. He had a thin moustache; his suit was very ordinary, shiny. He looked old-fashioned. His face was hard but his attitude was friendly, like a closed knife is friendly. His voice was London, South London, where the best crooks come from. He was about fifty years old.

"You'd better tell Billy Jay to take it slowly," he said, "tell him he stands no chance against the Bunce unless he has help, my help."

"I'll tell him," I said, "who are you?" I felt clumsy, as if the cameras were rolling and I was acting badly. A second take of the whole evening would have been welcome.

"Doesn't matter," he said, and he glanced around the room. He wasn't scared, just looking. "Tell Billy Jay what I told you . . . he'll need help with the Bunce, he has no idea what he's into."

The man turned and walked straight towards the automatic plate-glass doors. For him, they opened.

"What's the Bunce?" I asked, but he was outside by the time I had. A big black Ford moved up to him, a door opened, he ducked down into the car and was driven away.

I looked around me. There was just one girl in her orange uniform, sitting behind the reception counter. The lifts came and went or stood open and still. I began to think I was as mad as Billy; conspiracies everywhere, killers in the wardrobes.

Billy appeared beside me next. He must have tipped Eunice into bed and ridden the express lift back to find me. He was as pale as death, I could hear the blood from his face swilling about in his boots. He crowded up to me and grabbed the front of my jacket to stop me running away. That was twice in a quarter of an hour that I'd wanted to run away. He dragged me into a corner, away from the receptionist, my feet scuffled over the shaggy oatmeal carpet. "Right," said Billy between his teeth and not letting go of me, "what do you think you're doing, you untrustworthy little bastard?"

Billy wasn't good at being discreet and, when the receptionist looked up she saw a five-foot-six, ten-stone man dangling from the arm of an eighteen-stone, six-foot-eight man. She looked away.

"I'm not doing anything," I said, tearing weakly with both my hands at Billy's wrist. "What d'yer mean?"

"That man," said Billy, and he shook me.

"He just came over and talked, I've never seen him before tonight, never. He gave me a message for you."

"What was it?"

"For Christ's sake, Billy, put me down. I'm on your side."

Billy kept good hold of my jacket and pulled me into a sofa. "What message?" His eyes were narrow with needle.

"He said to be very careful, that you couldn't hope to take on the Bunce by yourself, you needed help, his help."

"Was he with the others, from the restaurant?"

"I don't know . . . I think he meant Old Nasty when he said the Bunce, that's who he meant. He sounded friendly."

"Friends like that I need like a third mortgage. What did he mean, the Bunce?"

"I don't know."

Billy released me at last and I tucked my shirt in under my belt. He leant back and hid the oval head in his big hands and used them to rub his eyes. When he'd finished, his face was red and worried.

"Do you know who that guy was, the one who gave you the message?"

I straightened my collar, glad that he wasn't going to hit me, and I gave him my honest face. "No, Billy, I've never seen him before. I told you, he wouldn't even give me his name."

Billy considered me for a while and then accepted that I was telling the truth. "During the getaway, when I was in the luton, that man was the only one I got a good look at, he's the one that got away, he's the fifth man. They're after me, got to be."

"Come on, Billy, then why this warning about Nasty, about the Bunce, if he wanted to get you he wouldn't be warning you, would he?"

Billy smiled at me from a great height. "That's the oldest con-trick in the world, the softening up technique, like the nice cop and the tough cop. Nasty is the Mr. Big behind Mr. Moustache. They've lost a lot of money because I was in the luton, now they want to cut their losses, squeeze some money out of me. Hundred thousand isn't bad money, you know, tide them over until their next job. I know how the underworld works, remember, you know it makes sense."

"No, Billy," I said, but it did make a kind of sense.

Billy leant forward. "You'll have to watch my back," he said seriously, just like someone out of a western.

I felt embarrassed. "Don't go over the top, Billy."

He grabbed me again. "Who's over the top? More than a million pounds' worth of gear is stolen, I shop the gang and the next thing I know the ring-leader is in my hotel. I suppose you think he wants to give me a booktoken for my granny?"

"It's unbelievable."

"I'm not asking you to believe it, just follow me around and keep your eyes open."

"But it's too far-fetched, isn't it? I mean, too ridiculous?"

"All right," said Billy, "so is a reward of a hundred thousand pounds ridiculous. But I want it, I need it, I deserve it and I'm going to get it."

CHAPTER ELEVEN
Goodbye Eunice

Breakfast was a banquet. The excitement and danger of meeting Nasty had made Billy heroic. He was Lord Byron at the head of the table the next morning, with Eunice on his right hand. There was nothing he couldn't deal with, no one he couldn't vanquish. He was brimming with an unreasonable certainty.

The *Mirror* article helped too. Half of the front page was given over to Billy and there was a photo of him, grinning outside the hotel. "Road Show Manager Foils Raiders," it said.

Kevin and the riggers had reappeared during the night and were going to sleep in our beds and bathe in our bathrooms while we worked. One of them got up and walked all the way round the breakfast table to slap Billy on the back. "You cracked it, boy," he said, "you cracked it."

Max was at breakfast too, sitting at a table, with his men within touching distance. He took the newspaper when it came to him and read it, and he didn't like what he saw. He could work out for himself that Billy had not been to Liverpool as I had pretended. Max gave me a hard look just to let me know he knew and that glance made me feel like an oven-ready chicken in a microwave cooker. He handed the newspaper back to me and congratulated Billy, but he wasn't happy.

The show, Pioneer Conference No. 1, was due to roll at two o'clock, after the audience had lunched. We were ready but Max wanted us to rehearse that morning to make sure. He had a new speech to give the Morley trainees, the new "Instructors," and at the end of it he listed all the Morley qualities: Compassion, Tenderness, Understanding, Integrity, Friendship, Endeavour, Generosity. As Max called forth these qualities, they were to appear through the drawbridge as men and women carrying huge crimson and white banners, each banner bearing the appropriate motto until, in the end, the stage would bristle with Max's words. "Let's get it right," he said, in the voice he used for opening envelopes, "I don't want those dummies running on stage with 'Excellence,' when I'm bawling out 'Achievement.'"

The show went well and afterwards the audience stood obediently in their places. Max waved his arms and the Morley Pioneers moved in and carried everyone off to seminar rooms for long practice sessions. Wherever you went that afternoon and evening you could hear the steady noise of work vibrating in the corridors.

Billy ran away with Eunice as soon as he was free, first to a drinking club and then to the most expensive restaurant he could find. The riggers broke the set and within four hours, the pantechnicon and Panurge were loaded and we might have left Nottingham there and then. But there was no need to move on. It took twenty-four hours for the Pioneers to move everything Max carried with him: typewriters, files, teleprinters. The next presentation was not due until Day 17 in Newcastle. Magic Lantern could relax and stay where it was until morning.

The rest of us did not follow Billy's example. We washed, loafed around the hotel, ate in the same old coffee shop and took our food from the same surly waitresses. Later on we watched the television films and listened to Jim going baroque about Eunice's body. Pretty early on we followed each other into a lift and pressed the button for bed. Only Duggie spoke as we surged upwards. "What's 'Diver,' Jim, in Portuguese?" he said. No one answered.

Outside the lift Duncan and Duggie walked down a different tunnel to Jim and me. "Goodnight," we said, and waved our hands. I followed Jim and we passed Billy's room. There were no lights on and his door was still off its hinges. I stopped outside my number and slipped the key into the lock. "See you tomorrow, Jim," I said. "Sleep well."

DAY 15

The phone woke me at half-past four. I looked at my watch and went for the receiver all in the same movement. My mind slipped a beat; I didn't know if it was the morning or the afternoon, yesterday or tomorrow. No light came through the curtains. I guessed it was the same night; no one would have allowed me to oversleep. If it was the afternoon I would have been in Newcastle. It was probably an alarm call gone wrong. It wasn't, it was Billy.

His voice was uneven and I could hear Eunice crying in the background. I'd never heard her sob before, I hadn't thought she could. "Come round here, right away," said Billy, and put the phone down. I dressed and went along, lifting the door aside to get into the room.

There was nothing much to see but the room felt extinguished, like a town where they'd been experimenting with germ warfare. Eunice was sitting on the carpet, with a face as desolate as an empty car-park. She was still crying, and Billy, in his dressing-gown, leant against the wall. His face too had decayed at the edges.

He motioned for me to sit and to be quiet. He ran a bath for Eunice and wheeled her into it with a glass of gin. Then he came back, shutting the bathroom door behind him.

"Nasty was here," he said, "with his friends." Then Billy sat down and told me his story and I believed it straight away.

Very late, and very drunk, Eunice and he had come back to the hotel. They couldn't get the lights to go on and Billy had

Goodbye Eunice

thought of ringing maintenance but decided against it; they hadn't even mended the door.

Eunice was already in bed by the time Billy joined her.

He took a deep breath; telling me the story wasn't easy but there was no one else he could tell.

"I said a lot of silly things in bed, like we all do: 'Eunice, I love you darling, I'm trapped without you, you keep me alive . . . ,' you know, on and on until it was over and then I went to sleep."

Billy lit a cigarette, took a deep lungful, blew it out, looked at both sides of his right hand and then continued with his story:

"I don't know how long I'd been asleep but suddenly all the lights came on and I woke up. I turned over to switch the lights off and, Jesus, there was Nasty and his four orang-outangs, sitting on those chairs."

I looked, and there were the chairs, abandoned in a semi-circle round the bed.

"It was horrible," said Billy. He shook his big head and dogged his cigarette. "Horrible. I got up, they let me get to my feet, they let me get into my dressing-gown, they let me shout . . . and then two of them hit me, at once." Billy pulled open his robe and showed me the marks. He was a big man, strong, with plenty of heart, but those men were very talented and they'd hurt Billy.

"I fell back onto the bed," he said, "I couldn't move. I've never been hit like that, never. They hit me a few more times, then they woke Eunice."

It was only five o'clock in the morning but I stood up and poured myself one of Billy's gins. I didn't know what was coming but I knew it wasn't going to be pleasant. Billy took my drink as I sat down, so I made another.

"Do you know, Mike," he said, "they'd been in the room all the time we were making love." His eyes shifted across mine, not locking. I didn't blame him and made no attempt to hold his gaze. "And they'd recorded the whole thing." He pointed, and there was the tape deck, there was the mike above the bed. Billy went over and gave me a minute or two of it. It was all there, the whole session, noises, screams, endearments; hideous, who'd want to listen to that stuff twice?

Billy switched the tape off. "They played it, all of it and made us listen, and they sat there and listened too, like it was their favourite comedy programme, only they didn't smile. I tried to get up to turn it off but they just hit me again. I thought they would rape Eunice then, not that I was worried for her, she could have seen them all off . . ."

"Did they?" I asked.

Billy shook his head. "No, it was worse." He stumbled over his words, embarrassed, but he went on. "When the tape came to an end, one of them got up and broke the end off one of the gin bottles, grabbed Eunice by the hair and held the jagged end right up to her face."

I looked at the carpet and saw the broken pieces; in the wastepaper basket were the remains of the bottle.

"Eunice tried to twist her head away . . . but he was too strong . . . she couldn't even scream, she was whimpering, like a puppy run over by a truck." Billy dropped his head and cleared his throat. "Then the man said, 'All right, Eunice, let's see you do a nice blow-job.'"

Billy lifted his head and smiled the palest smile.

"You mean, with them?" I said.

"No, with me. I mean it was somehow . . . I mean . . . an audience of five, not even friends."

"And you did?"

"'You'll do it,' the man said, 'or I'll take her face off.' We did it. Eunice has got a nice face . . . she didn't want to lose it, she'll make the big-time one day. She did it and someone took photographs."

We fell silent again and Billy sipped his gin.

"The worst thing," he said after a while, "was that we'd only just finished . . . and with them watching, it wouldn't work . . . you know. Poor Eunice, she kept trying . . . I've never felt so low in my life . . . and then, in the middle of it all, they just got up and walked out." Billy bit his lip and looked away from me, raising the back of his hand to his eyes.

"Let them have the money, Billy," I said, "that's what they want, we're not in their league. They know about getting their own way. They're going to get it in the end, let them have it."

Billy rose from his chair. "No," he said, "not now, I've earned it. It's mine." He went into the bathroom to see how Eunice was and I swallowed some of my drink.

It was half-past five, now, the dawn was up though I could still see lights flashing on the motorway. Billy came back. "What are you going to do?" I asked him.

"I'm going to call the law, put them onto it. Nasty's part of the Heathrow gang and he's after my money. I'd be stupid to keep quiet. I didn't want to shop those guys in the first place, I'm glad I have now."

"What about Eunice?"

"I'll send her home, out of the way. They're not after her, it's not even me they want, it's only the money."

DAY 15

CHAPTER TWELVE

A Bumpy Road to Newcastle

They came while we were having breakfast. There were two of them. Billy and I had said nothing to the others about Nasty's night-time visit, so when they arrived at our table Billy took them, with Eunice and me, to a quiet corner of reception.

They were fresh-faced young policemen in good suits and they looked very sympathetic. They didn't laugh when Billy told his story, though Billy did, to cover his embarrassment. Eunice nodded when she had to and smoked her cigarettes. I said I'd seen the evidence in the room.

The policemen took descriptions of Nasty, his friends and of the fifth man from the Heathrow robbery. They agreed that it all seemed to tie in very closely with the hold-up and that the reward might have something to do with it. They stood up at last, put their notebooks away and asked where we were going next. "Hamilton Towers, Newcastle," said Billy, and they said, "Fine." Before they left, I went upstairs with them to see the room and the broken bottle. They got their men to go over the place for finger-prints even though Billy had told them that Nasty's men had worn white gloves of cotton, like film editors. They also wanted to play the tape.

The policemen shook hands and said they were sorry that it had happened, sorry that it had happened on their patch.

They sounded sincere and I liked them. They'd be in touch, they said. When it was over Billy put Eunice into a cab for the airport, and the last I saw of her was her pale and perfect face, gone in an instant. The incomprehension in her eyes was pathetic and it was the only time I ever liked her.

We set off for Newcastle. I rode with Billy in the Volvo and the three others shared the bench seat in the van. I hated motoring with Billy, but he allowed me to drive so he could sleep and it wasn't too bad.

I coasted the Volvo down the hotel ramp and slotted her into a summery morning on the motorway. Blue exhaust smoke stood solid a yard or so above the surface of the concrete and I drove with the windows up. I overtook Panurge and went hard until I reached the service area about half way to Newcastle. I eased the car through the lorries and parked. Billy and I got out and leant against the Volvo in the sun, waiting for the others, listening to the road.

We waited a long while, an hour, two hours. I wanted to get on ahead and eat, but Billy insisted on standing there. Apart from that, it was a nice day.

At last the truck bowled across the car-park and stopped in front of us. I looked up and reminded myself that Ken Hutchins would need to paint in another swastika for Casey Roberts. The boys had a bad story to tell. They had been stopped three times along the way by police patrols and they'd been given a very hard time.

"They kept us for hours," said Duncan, "opened the back, all the documents, looked at the tyres, we had to unload half the gear twice and prove that we hadn't nicked it."

"They were sods," said Duggie, he was very angry. "You know how they can niggle, so polite, so superior; bastards!"

We walked over to the restaurant together.

"Those guys in the third patrol car looked like the guys in the first car to me," said Jim, "but I couldn't believe it, they wouldn't make a mistake like that, would they?"

Billy looked at me; "They would if they wanted to," he said.

The restaurant bridged the motorway itself, and as we ate we could watch the cars and trucks throwing themselves out of sight below. There were occasional glimpses, too, of the drivers, clinging to their steering-wheels, their faces white and baleful. On the way back to the car Billy pulled me away from the others.

"They weren't coppers," he whispered, "they were some of Nasty's pals, dressed as coppers, they said it would be easy to sabotage the show. Imagine what Max would do to me if we started setting the show up two or three hours late. He still owes me half the money, he could break Magic Lantern just by hanging on to his cheque."

Billy let the truck get half an hour in front of us, then followed after it, fast; he was driving, and sober. I sat next to him, my safety-belt tight and hanging onto the rim of my seat with both hands.

We came over a high hill on the motorway and saw the long swoop, down and up, of a rolling valley, miles of it. A three-lane highway on each side and toy trucks and cars burning up and down the country. It was impressive. Panurge was at the bottom of a five-mile slope, pulled over on the hard shoulder, the shutter was up and a policeman was standing watching the boys while they handed out some of the gear. He had his back towards us, his motorbike was on its stand behind him.

Billy laughed. He let the Volvo roll in with the engine off. With all the noise of passing trucks, the copper didn't realise that we'd arrived. Jim was up in the van, handing things down to Duncan and Duggie. He saw the Volvo stop, he saw Billy get out and come towards Panurge on his toes. Jim didn't flicker an eyelid, he didn't smile, he went on unloading and talking to the policeman. I stayed in my seat and watched.

Billy grabbed the policeman round the neck and lifted him off the ground and shook him. For a short while I thought Billy was going to kill him, but he only shook the man until he collapsed. The hard shoulder was high above the fields and

Billy carried his victim to the edge of the tarmac and threw him, as far as he could. The policeman's boots flashed in the sun, he landed about half way down the slope and then rolled to the bottom and lay still. I got out of the car.

Duncan was horrified. "They can put you into prison for that, Billy." He was pale, pale enough to make me think he was going to be sick.

"That was the fourth bastard," said Duggie, "and he was worse than the others."

The radio transmitter on the bike made a noise and Jim dropped from the back of the lorry and demolished it with an adjustable spanner.

Duncan stared at us, his eyes rigid. "You're all crazy, we'll get run in for this, they'll have the number of the van, they'll be onto us."

Billy cackled. "These guys aren't coppers, Dunc, I promise you, they're the same guys as did the Heathrow job, they had a go at me last night, and the night before. I know who they are."

Jim nodded down the embankment to where the policeman was making flapping movements with his arms. "It'll be bloody funny if you're wrong, Billy," he said. "I mean, coppers are generally coppers, aren't they?"

Billy jerked the bike off its stand and pushed it off the edge of the road. It rolled on its wheels a little way and then fell over, slithering and churning to a stop in the grass. "They are crooks, dressed as coppers," he said.

"I don't care, you don't catch me driving the van," said Duncan, "not now."

"All right," said Billy, "drive the Volvo, I'll take the van. If this guy turns out to be a real copper, then you haven't done anything, have you? I threw him over, not you, and the bike."

Duncan didn't say another word but walked to the car, Duggie went with him. I made a good try at getting into the shooting-brake too, but Billy wouldn't wear it. "You come with me," he said, "I may need a witness, and you're the only person, apart from me, who knows what's going on."

Jim didn't seem worried either way. "I'll go along with you, Billy," he said, "I'm not scared of the bleeders, coppers or not. I'll stretch out in the luton and have a quick Jodrell as we go. Any drink in the fridge?" and he clambered up the open door of the truck, pulled open the flap and crawled out of sight.

Billy leant over the big driving-wheel and lifted Panurge up the map, getting ten miles per hour more out of the truck than I could. There was a hopeful look on his face but nobody stopped us, nobody came. Lorries and cars went by, brake lights shone red and indicators exploded like fireworks. Faces passed, rushing down the road. Up above in the luton, Jim relaxed and switched on the intercom to listen to Billy and me, but we had nothing to say so he made himself a gin and told us about the Oxfordshire painting job: it was his folk song.

"I used to be in building," he said, "house-painting mainly. It was pretty well paid, not as good as this, though. The best job I ever had was redecorating this farmhouse. Lovely it was, Oxfordshire, owned by this woman, about thirty, three kids, private schools, horse-riding, five cars, the lot. I was only eighteen then, young. Her name was Thresher. I wasn't the only fella working there, mind, on the farmhouse, I mean, but she took to me, must have. Her husband went off to the City every day, pots of money they had. The farm itself was worth a million they reckoned, they'd bought it for an investment, she said, rented out the fields.

"I'd only been there a couple of days before she sussed me out. Fed me on the best food, I've never eaten like that before: oysters, jugged hare, getting me strength up, she was. I never wanted to leave it, the farmhouse I mean. I had the run of the place, beautiful bathrooms, lovely gardens, swimming pool. She used to like having it done in the garden, she was an active bird. Liked to get me at it when she was on the telephone to her husband at work. Knockout, that was.

"Course, the other decorators didn't like me getting paid full whack just for gamming Mrs. Thresher, but she squared that with the foreman and she was dropping me so much money that I could afford to bribe everyone within a radius of ten miles. I had to work for it, mind, but it was a pleasure."

Jim went silent for a while, just thinking, then he went on: "Still it couldn't last for always. The old man started coming home unexpected, him in his bloody coffee-coloured Range Rover, with the personalised number plates, DON 1, or some such. Still, that's the advantage of those big houses, that is. By the time he'd found out which room we were in, she had her drawers back on and I'd had time to whip a brush out the turps and find a window to paint. With half a dozen blokes in white overalls all over the place, her husband didn't stand a chance of finding out which one of us was working on his wife. "Hello, darling," she used to say, "my golly, you're 'ome early."

"He nearly caught us one afternoon, though, in the garden. There wasn't a lot I could pretend to paint out there, greenhouse, I suppose. Anyway, the job came to an end, they finished the decorating. She gave me eighty quid when I left, cash too, and a gold lighter. Cried her eyes out, she did. 'You'll have to come back, in the week,' she said, 'when I'm alone, try and ring me up.' I did, of course, but it was never convenient, that's what she said. Bloody shame. Paradise it was. Never met anyone like her . . . well, like her, yes, but not so rich."

Two-thirds of the way to Newcastle I took over the driving. Billy drank some wine for a while and then went to sleep in the other corner of the cab. The lanes of concrete rose and fell across the wide fields, going northwards. It was a road that didn't give a damn about anyone, anything. At last, a notice said the next exit was mine. Behind me stretched a switchback of trucks and cars, all the way to London. The motorway began to climb towards my exit and I shifted my grip on the wheel.

In the mirror I saw a blue truck move into the middle lane, going fast. Behind that, further back along the curve of the highway, a white police car, a Jaguar. Another notice went by and told me that I had one mile to go. The road still climbed and I pressed my right foot to the floor, but Panurge was already giving all there was. Billy slept on. Another sign, exit half a mile. The blue truck moved up on me until its cab was level with my tail, the white car moved up with it. Exit three hundred yards. I indicated left. The blue truck came on, he indicated, and the white car dropped behind him. Exit two hundred yards, one hundred yards.

The slip road soared steeply and peeled left, leaving the solid lanes of traffic to drop away and out of my sight. I was driving across a man-made hill, and a hundred and fifty feet below me were a couple of scraggy fields with four Friesians standing stock still in them, like plywood adverts for milk. Beyond some more fields and a stand of trees I could see the towers of our hotel.

Mirror again; the blue truck was overtaking, right here, on the two-lane exit. Mad sod! Right behind me now I caught a glimpse of the white police car. The blue truck came level with me, it was big, a breakdown truck, the kind they use to tow juggernauts and trailers. It roared its diesel engine, and the push of its slipstream levered Panurge towards the thin fencing that stood on the edge of the embankment.

The driver of the other vehicle looked over at me and grinned. He was in blue overalls; underneath them I spied a dark tunic with silver buttons. I twisted my steering-wheel and brought Panurge away from the hard shoulder. The other man drew ahead and I eased my foot from the accelerator to let him go. Big white letters slowly crept past my cab window, painted three feet high on the side of the truck, they spelt POLICE. I was dropping back, in a second I'd be overtaken.

Jim came on the mike from the luton and said, "Where are we?"

"Nearly there," I shouted. I was shouting because I was scared. I yelled at Billy to come awake but he didn't.

"What's up, Mike?" said Jim's voice.

"There's someone overtaking," I said, "driving like a maniac."

The blue truck was three-quarters past me and I thought it was over. It wasn't. I caught a glimpse of the other driver in his mirror; wavy blond hair, young looking, white teeth. Taking his time, he swerved and nudged me. Panurge staggered, my insides shifted violently with fear and I was onto the hard shoulder. I swayed back onto the roadway and stamped for the brake. As I slowed down, the blue truck went for me again, changing lanes as if I weren't there, using weight to push Panurge off the road.

I grabbed the steering-wheel hard and I stood, upright, on the brake, but Panurge was already through the fencing, skidding into the air. There was hardly any noise and I felt disembodied for a second. Then the horizon tipped over like a framed landscape falling off a wall, and down it went, crooked.

Billy was flung tighter into his corner and wedged there, clutching his wine bottle. I dropped towards him and my face went close to his face and I saw him wake up, surprised. I tried to hold onto his arm but the summer sky swivelled across the windscreen. I went weightless again but the weight returned with twice its strength and smashed me down into the controls. Again the sky pivoted, the bottle broke and Panurge fell.

Jim called out, "What the hell's going on?"

We rolled over and I screamed, "Oh, God!" I heard Jim shout once more, "Shit!" and that was the last thing I heard, because Billy was thrown at me then and my head hit something hard, the roof of the cab, maybe, and I went out. It was the last thing I ever heard Jim say, because when I woke it was to learn that the Greenford "Diver" was dead. They found him lying half in and half out of the shattered luton, his back broken and his mouth full of blood.

DAY 15

CHAPTER THIRTEEN
The Bunce

I opened my eyes and saw Billy in bed. I was in bed too, up to my neck in sheets as stiff as sandpaper. We were in a private room of the Newcastle General Hospital and Billy lay back on his pillows, staring. I studied him, looking for injuries. My knowledge of medicine comes from television serials and, as his legs weren't suspended from the ceiling, I assumed that he wasn't badly hurt. His face was lopsided though, with blue and yellow patches under each eye. He looked beaten and bruised.

The sight of him made me think of myself and my head started throbbing as soon as I did. I raised my hand and found bandages wrapped around my skull; the outside of my head was tender, inside it hurt. I wriggled my fingers and toes and they all worked. My right arm and all my ribs were sore.

I looked for the door to the room and found it on my left. It was half glass, led into a dark corridor, and on the other side of it stood a policeman in uniform. Heavy curtains were drawn across the room's one window and it was impossible to tell whether it was night or day. I closed my eyes. The door opened, making a noise like a harp, and the policeman came in and went to Billy's bed. I watched him through a flickering eyelid. Billy broke his stare and the policeman said, "Well, how are you then, all right?"

"Fine," said Billy, "are you for real?"

The policeman took out his warrant card and showed it to Billy, who said, "Nice, what else did you get for Christmas?"

"Who was driving?" said the policeman, sitting down.

"He was." Billy moved his head in my direction. "I was too drunk."

"Yes, that's what the blood-test said; but according to the crew of our police car, when they got down to your truck you were in the driving seat."

"The way we were rolling about," said Billy, "I could have been found with the gear lever up me Khyber. He was driving, he'll tell you that when he comes round."

"I'm sure he will, but that won't prove anything, will it?" He paused. "I have to confirm the name of the deceased."

"Jim . . . James O'Reilly, 22 Goldfinch Lane, Greenford. That's London."

"Yes, that's what I've got. Next of kin are being informed."

"Poor sods!" said Billy.

I turned over, still pretending to be asleep. I jerked my head under a pillow and pulled it below the bedclothes.

That was how I learnt that Jim was dead.

"Do you want to make a statement yet? No . . . very wise, you're probably in shock. There may be a prosecution, dangerous and drunken driving, at least. You know, it's hard to see how you escaped alive. The officers on the spot said you drove straight off the road, they even found bottles of wine in the cab."

"I wasn't driving," said Billy. "I won't say any more. Did you give him a blood-test?"

"Oh yes, he's in the clear, he is."

"That's fine, then, I've phoned my office, my wife is on her way, so is my solicitor. We'll make full statements when he gets here, in front of the proper people."

I looked out from under my pillow. The policeman nodded, "Very wise, very wise," he said. He stood up straight and tucked his chin tidily into his neck. "I shall have to come back before long, I hope it doesn't turn into manslaughter."

He turned, and the studs of his shoes scraped the clean floor.

I sat up. "It was me driving," I said, "and it was one of your bloody trucks that forced us off the road, we wouldn't have crashed but for that."

Billy looked at me angrily; I was surprised. The policeman ignored what I'd said.

"Oh, you've come round, then? That is good, we were worried about you, but you mustn't think you can help him by taking the blame yourself, we've had that one pulled on us before, you know. It was Mr. Jay who drove off the road, there were police witnesses right behind him in a patrol car. I was one of them. It was me that called the ambulance."

I stared at the man. I couldn't understand.

"You're mad," I said, "there was a blue truck, forced us off the road. There must be other witnesses." I looked at Billy but he seemed untroubled. He showed me the palms of his hands and raised his shoulders.

The policeman laid his hand on the door-knob. "I'm afraid no one stopped, apart from us. You know how it is, people are pretty callous, besides we were waving them on. They don't like to get involved, might have to come miles to a hearing, inconvenient, no one stopped anyway. What blue truck?" He smiled at me, powerful and untouchable.

"What have you done with Jim?" I asked.

The policeman looked sad. "He's in the fridge, downstairs."

"What about the blue truck, then? It was one of yours, it had POLICE written on the side."

The policeman inclined his head politely and said nothing.

"Go on," said Billy, "piss off before I put you in the fridge too." The policeman smiled again and left; the spring in the door made its harp noise. When it stopped, I said, "I know I was driving, Billy, whatever that copper says. I'm not crazy, there was a blue truck, a police truck and it pushed me off the road. For Christ's sake, didn't you see anything before we went over?"

Billy laughed. "No," he said, "not a thing, but it doesn't matter."

"What do you mean, 'it doesn't matter.' If the coppers say you were driving, that you were drunk and that you're responsible for Jim, you could end up doing time. It would finish you, what would happen to Magic Lantern then?"

Billy looked smug. "You dummy," he said, "that guy who just went out of here was not a real copper, the police car behind us was not a real police car, and the blue truck was not a police truck. They were all working for Nasty."

"You're saying that this last copper wasn't a copper?"

"If you can dress up for a robbery you can dress for anything."

"I didn't just drive off the road, there was a blue truck."

"Sure there was, Nasty's. He said he'd sabotage the show and he has."

"Poor Jim," I said.

"Yeah, it's incredible."

I touched the bandages on my head. "This whole thing's getting very Kafka."

Billy looked at me suspiciously.

The accident had happened about lunchtime on Day 15, and we'd been admitted to Newcastle General an hour or so later. I'd come out of the crash with slight concussion and cuts. Billy had been conscious all the time, protected from serious injury by being drunk, though he had sobered up rapidly in the ambulance, his mind concentrated by the need to save the show. The more he was up against it, the better Billy worked.

On arrival at the hospital he'd ordered a private room and had begun telephoning immediately, first to Fran, so that she could assemble all the stand-by material, and then to Duncan and Duggie, sending them back to the scene of the crash with instructions to salvage everything they could; cable, slides, machines. When they knew what gear was irreparable, they were to make a list and bring it directly to Billy's bedside.

While I had lain unconscious, he had organised everything and placated everyone. He had phoned Fran again, with his list, telling her to hire replacement personnel and equipment through Shaw, Nichols Associates, another firm in the same line of business. When she'd done that, Billy wanted her and Jonathan Lane, his solicitor, to fly to Newcastle. Fran would travel with the gear and supervise its transport; not one thing was to be forgotten and not one thing was to be lost.

Next, Billy had phoned Max and told him the Morley timetable would remain unaltered. The next show, scheduled for 14:30, Day 17, would run on time. The riggers had the main set up already; Duncan and Duggie had ample time for technical run-throughs on all the modules; the electricians were getting the lamps into working order, they could also rig Jim's control board; a relief operator was flying up from London and Fran could stand by to stage-manage just in case I hadn't recovered in time.

Max wasn't a bit worried about these technicalities. He knew he could count on things working as long as Billy was alive, but he was frightened that Billy might die. Within ten minutes of the telephone call, Max had appeared at the hospital, three of his aides were negotiating for a permanent line between Billy and the Morley Office, and special menus with private nursing twenty-four hours a day had been arranged. Max had taken Billy's pulse himself, called for the house-surgeon, and only when he had been assured several times that Billy was out of all danger had the anguish left his face.

"Can't run the show without you, kid," he had said, ruffling Billy's hair with his fat hand. "You take good care, now; take it easy, you've done all you can." And off he'd gone.

"Did he ask about me?" I wondered.

Billy smirked. "He didn't even notice that you were in the same room," he said, "but one of his aides did."

I looked at my watch; 21:00, Day 15. It would be one of those spacious and cool evenings of summer outside, with everywhere going grey, slowly, as the sun went down. Billy talked into the phone and I dozed. A nurse appeared and said something; Billy got her by the hand and slipped her a tenner and she went out. Billy talked on and I fell asleep, only to wake an hour or so later when I heard a voice I recognised saying, "Is he out?"

"Yes," answered Billy, "concussion, sleeps all the time." Billy's voice had gone royal again, high and forced, pretending not to be frightened. I half opened my eyes and saw a man standing midway between Billy's bed and mine. He was holding a bunch of red roses in one hand and an automatic in the other. He looked like a colour poster for a florists with a new line in pushing sales. The bouquet and the gun were pointed at Billy. I closed my eyes; the man holding the gun was the man who had held my elbow in the Nottingham hotel. Same hair, same face, same shiny suit. I opened half an eye.

He gave the flowers to Billy and Billy held them under his nose. "Thanks," he said.

"They don't smell much," said the man, "they're vulgar flowers, really, but that's all they had outside on the barrow."

Billy dropped the roses into his jug of orange-juice. It looked like a studied defiance and might have been impressive, except his hand was shaking.

"Don't upset yourself about the gun," said the man. "I just don't want you to ring bells or start shouting or get violent, you look stronger than I am, younger."

I watched Billy's face; you couldn't blame him for being scared. The man whose robbery he'd ruined was sitting at his bedside, with a gun in his lap.

"You do this charity work in your spare time?" asked Billy.

"No," said the man, "I don't like hospitals, they're too much like prisons. You never know what they are going to do to you next, do you?" He glanced over towards me but I stayed resolutely asleep. "I've come to talk to you, Billy . . . you've slipped into more trouble than you know about."

"I saw you at Waddestone," said Billy, "the fuzz didn't pick you up?"

"Sheer luck I was out. You spoilt a decent little job, lost me a lot of money and there'll be more work to do before I'm finished." There was no anger in the man's voice, just disappointment.

"I'm sorry," Billy said, and his apology should have sounded stupid but he meant it. He really was sorry, he didn't like messing up someone else's work. He leant over to the cabinet by his bed and pulled open the door and the man raised his gun. Very carefully, Billy showed him that all he had in the cupboard was a quart of gin and a bottle of lemonade. He must have sent the nurse for it. "Would you like some?"

The man nodded and I saw the skull of his bullet head gleam under the hair-oil. Billy passed over a drink. "What's your name?"

"Rosser," said the man, "Rosser." He sipped. "Nice," he added, and leant back in his chair. "Are you quite sure that yours was the information that led to the capture of the men who did the Heathrow job?"

Billy hesitated. "There was nothing personal, it was just an accident that I was in the truck."

"And my tankful of petrol," said Rosser, "was that an accident?"

Billy was caught off-balance and I was amazed to see him blush. Rosser raised a hand. "Answer my question, were you the only informant the law had?"

"Yes," said Billy, "I know I was. A friend of mine works for the *Daily Mirror*. He was at the police-station when they brought your men in, he told me the police were nowhere until they got that tip-off from me." He looked nervously at Rosser's gun. "I'm sorry."

"Right, now suppose the police argued that in fact they got their tip-offs from two informers in the Trade and it was them who deserved the reward. What would you say to that?"

"The Trade?"

"The Trade is where the police world and the criminal world overlap, where they work together."

"Well, if the law say that then they say it, how would I know?"

Rosser leant forward, "Exactly, how would you know?"

There was silence. It was as if Rosser had said all he wanted to say on the subject. I expected him to get up and walk out.

"Well?" said Billy.

"Who are the insurance companies going to believe if you quarrel with John Law about who gets the reward?"

"The law, of course."

"Precisely." Rosser let another long silence go by.

Billy broke into it. "I'd fight it though, I'd get lawyers, I'd make them work for it."

"Yes, and you'd end up spending more money than you might stand to gain, and you'd have a lot of aggro and a lot of parking tickets all of a sudden. Face it, in normal circumstances if you were offered any kind of reward, you'd cop the money and shut up."

Billy nodded.

Rosser went on, "That's what most people do—only these aren't normal circumstances, you're greedy and that man who came to see you in Nottingham, you hit him!"

"He threatened my show, I'd hit anyone who did that."

"Where's your show now? Pushed off the road by a big blue truck."

"There was a blue truck?"

"That's right, there was a blue truck. You shouldn't have lost your temper with the man from Vauxhall Insurance, he only came to tell you that other people might be claiming some of the reward."

"I'd drunk a fair bit."

Rosser held his glass out for some more gin. "He's a proud man, being smacked by you would make him very angry. You're lucky this is all he's done to you."

"It isn't," said Billy, and he told Rosser a little about Nasty and Eunice.

"Nasty's a good name," said Rosser, "a very good name."

Billy sat up in his bed, looked at Rosser and did one of the bravest things he'd ever done, he called Rosser a liar. "Rosser," he said, "I think you and Nasty set up the Heathrow robbery. I ruined it and, because I ruined it, I stand to get a reward of between a hundred and a hundred and fifty thousand, maybe more. You want that money, both of you, and you don't care how you get it, you've got to cut your losses, like any business. Nasty plays nasty and you play nice, it's the old con. I think the coppers who buggered us about on the motorway were your guys, dressed as coppers, and I think the truck that pushed us off the road was your truck. You killed Jim, and if I can I'll see you and Nasty behind bars for it."

I tried to look even more asleep. I didn't want Rosser to think I'd heard all that. A nurse came to the door and twanged it open. Billy and Rosser both stared at her and she went away again.

Rosser took Billy's accusations very calmly. Billy offered him a cigarette and he refused. "Unhealthy," he said. Rosser seemed puzzled, as if he couldn't think how to convince Billy of what he wanted to say.

"You have an innocent view of life, Billy," he said at last. "Try listening to this scenario, quite simple, especially for someone who's in the business like you are." Rosser stretched his legs and settled himself more comfortably. "Let's say there's a big robbery, the insurance companies go mad, it's going to cost them a fortune in compensation, so they offer a hefty reward. Meanwhile, the law, all on their own, actually find the stuff. They round up the gang and the loot, everyone is happy, berserk, our policemen are wonderful. Wouldn't it be a pity if the reward went to waste; isn't it a shame there's no one claiming it. But wait!" Rosser said it like it was the caption in a silent movie. "Here comes honest Joe Soap, by chance a regular police informer—sometimes he's an ex-copper—he has heard the news. 'Of course,' says the officer in charge of the case, 'Mr. Soap gave us a great deal of useful information.' If the law says that Mr. Soap gave them the number of the gang's car, why should the insurers doubt them? They'll pay up with a smile."

Rosser turned his head slowly to look at me and I forgot to be asleep. "It's a good story, isn't it?" he said.

"It's incredible," said Billy.

"He's having us on." I sat up.

Rosser smiled, "Where have you old ladies been living? So, the insurance companies hand over the money to Joe Soap, who marches off to the nearest pub to celebrate his sudden rise to fortune . . . but he's not alone, he's got some old friends with him, to help carry the cash, old friends from the police force. They'll leave him a bit, of course, for himself, more than he could earn in a year or two. Joe will be thankful and he'll keep his mouth shut. He'll have to, otherwise he'll become a road accident statistic . . . like your friend Jim."

There was another long silence at that. Billy poured drinks all round and I got one, brought over by Rosser. He was a strange-looking man, such a hard face, yet somehow not unkind.

Rosser sat down again. "If the law picks up a large chunk of reward, say fifty or sixty grand, what do you think they'd do with it?"

"I don't know, share it out, spend it?"

"That's too rough and ready these days, Billy. Everyone in the game has to get a share proportionate to the amount of effort put in. From each according to their gains, to all according to their rank, we're not talking about a handful of bent coppers, and there's A10 to watch out for nowadays, some of them. If you're a copper you can't suddenly go out and buy a new car, a new house. Everyone knows what a copper earns and it's not much. And that's how the Bunce was born."

"The Bunce?"

"The Bunce. Look, there's a huge amount of money coming in every week, no one even knows how much; gambling, pornography, smuggling, illegal immigrants, drugs. No copper wants to be found with money in his pockets, it's incriminating. The money has to be got rid of, laundered, yet it has to be available too, in small amounts—preferably so that everyone gets it when he needs it. That damn money keeps growing, quiet and invisible, like grass under a paving stone. It's an embarrassment to everyone and so it goes into a fund, and from there it goes into things like insurance, shares, gilt-edged, some goes abroad."

"Oh come on," said Billy. He didn't look as certain as he sounded.

Rosser smiled. "The Bunce is big and it is legal. And the money is invested by men who know what they are doing; they are the Bunce and every copper who works for them across the country benefits from the Bunce and is part of it too."

"And you say this goes on all over?"

"Wherever there's a copper, there's the Bunce. It has the best equipment the tax-payer can buy; cars, radio, computers, helicopters. It is too strong to beat, it is simple and it is also generous to its friends."

"Generous?"

"Sure it is. If a Bunce copper gets put inside, his family is looked after for as long as it takes. Every now and then everyone who works for the Bunce sees a man arrive in a little cheap car with a bundle of cash in his hand, not too much, enough to double the wages."

"And is every copper part of the Bunce?" asked Billy, more interested now.

"No, and they don't have to be, but there's a huge passive membership, and a lot of affiliations. It's like urban terrorism, you only need a handful to make it work but there's more than a handful to the Bunce. It's like the Morley pyramid, put key men in key positions all the way up and there's nothing you can't achieve."

The Bunce

"You're telling us that a certain percentage of all the coppers in Britain are bent?"

Rosser laughed. "Of course it depends how you look at it. What's bent about putting extra money to good use? The whole world does it. It's free enterprise. If the Bunce claims your reward money, it's not really dishonest, sharp practice, maybe, so what?"

"It's dishonest to me," said Billy, "I want it."

Rosser drank from his glass and none of us spoke for a minute or two.

"What about those coppers I had round to the hotel at Nottingham, after the Eunice business, the ones I put onto Nasty, were they straight?"

"No reason why they shouldn't have been, but they'll get nowhere. It will take time, they'll find nothing, they'll be put onto something else, the papers will go adrift. Bureaucracy is an evergreen, Billy, and the Bunce lives in it."

"What about the coppers who made us unload the truck three times on the motorway, and the one I threw down the embankment . . . you're saying they were real coppers."

"Yes, and they won't say a word, they were on Bunce work."

"And the truck," I said, "the blue truck, the one that killed Jim, were they coppers too, loyal to the Bunce?"

Rosser nodded. "I don't think they meant that to happen, they wouldn't have known anyone was in the luton, they certainly wouldn't have known that Billy was in the van, he should have been driving the Volvo. As for you . . . expendable."

"But they killed Jim, just for money."

"One hundred and fifty thousand pounds is not just money."

Billy poured some more drinks. "If they have so much money, why do they want mine?"

"Lots of reasons. They have monthly figures and they like them to look good. Sometimes they need cash in a hurry, for something special. They like reward money best of all, it's nice and clean and they feel they've earned it. That's why the pressure is on you, Billy."

"Bugger the pressure," said Billy, leaning forward in his bed. "I won't let you scare me out of my reward with a cock and bull story. I won't give you a light."

"Billy," said Rosser patiently, "it's not me, and they'll get you in the end. You're so vulnerable, you've got all your life invested in Magic Lantern and they could smash it to bits by tomorrow morning."

"Crap," said Billy, "this is my one chance to get clear."

"You've no chance at all unless you throw in with me. I know the Trade, you don't, but I'd want half."

"No!"

Rosser stood up and placed his drink on the table. "It'll all be over in a few days, as soon as the property has been verified, as soon as the Loss Adjustor makes up his mind."

"And who's the Loss Adjustor?"

"He's the man employed on a temporary basis, by the insurance companies, to estimate how much, or how little, should be paid out in reward. He can come from anywhere in the insurance world but they tend to use someone they know, someone who's done it before. When the law puts the evidence in front of him, you'll be lucky to come out of it with ten grand. Invite me in and I'll see you get a lot more than that, fifty at least."

"No," said Billy. "First, I don't believe you; second, I want it all."

Rosser put his gun into his jacket pocket. "I can only give you a couple of days to think about it. I need money too." He moved towards the door. "Leave the time of Jim's funeral at reception, I'll see you there. Meanwhile, you do me a favour, and yourself; get your legal man to visit the Loss Adjustor and put in your claim, and find out what the total reward is likely to be and how many others are after it. And, when he's done all that, get your man to tell you what the Loss Adjustor looks like." He opened the door and it made its noise.

"Wait a minute," said Billy, "in this scenario of yours, where does Nasty fit in?"

Rosser threw back his head and really laughed. "I didn't dare start with that," he said. "Nasty is right at the top of the pile, Mr. Bunce himself, never goes anywhere without those four guys. He's the accountant."

Then Rosser was gone and the door went plunk behind him.

Billy rolled his head on his shoulder and looked across at me. "Well, what do you think about that?"

"I don't know," I said, "he seems a nice enough fellow, but then who knows what to think about anyone in this day and age?"

DAY 16

CHAPTER FOURTEEN

The Show Must Go On

Fran was sitting on Billy's bed when I woke up. It was eight o'clock in the morning and it was Day 16. I felt good and warm, rested, out of it, and I didn't want to go back. My pillow was wet with saliva. I wriggled upright and wiped my mouth. Fran came over and looked down at me and smiled and touched my hair. "Hello," she said.

I liked Fran, admired her too, but then so did everyone. She had been married to Billy for about five or six years, and anyone who could stay with him that long deserved as much admiration as she could get.

"Hello, Fran," I said. "Any breakfast?"

"It's on the way." She sat on the edge of my bed and looked at the floor. "Rotten about Jim; Billy told me. Some big lorry, and they haven't got it yet."

I glanced over her shoulder to where Billy sat, half dressed, on a wooden chair. His eyes glared danger at me; that meant he hadn't told her the half of it; nothing about the Bunce, nothing about Nasty.

"Poor Jim," I said.

"He always gave a girl hope," she said, "he used to spark off the most extraordinary fantasies, you might have all been killed. How do you feel?"

"I don't know yet . . . weak, trembly."

The Show Must Go On

Billy was nearly dressed. "The gear came up last night," he said. "I'm going in to check it through, we'll be rehearsing tonight, it's going to be all right, don't worry."

I laughed. Same old Billy. As if I gave a damn about the show apart from the wages. "I'm sure you'll manage one run without me."

"Easy," said Fran. "I'll be back-stage and Les Eastaugh has come up to take over the lighting. I've ordered you your best breakfast, bacon and tinned tomatoes."

Fran was amazing. Hundreds of people screamed through her house in a week and yet she always remembered what I ate and the fact that I took no milk in my tea. I saw her about four times a year.

Fran was just past thirty then and her face was a true revelation of herself, as it always is with good people. She smiled from a large mouth and there was nothing self-indulgent about it. Her face had good lines too, lots of them, all tired. It was a wonder she was still alive; living, driving and working with Billy, at his speed. She drank as much as he did, she had to; she smoked as much too, and she kept his awful hours and kept them every night.

Magic Lantern worked from two big Victorian houses on the north side of Clapham Common. Billy had gone into the houses, gutted them and made them into one house. They were now stuffed with recording studios and design rooms. The whole attic, glass-roofed, was given over to artwork and photography, and there were more rooms for slide mounting and editing. Billy had everything he needed to prepare and equip his shows, including a preview theatre. His cars lived in the garden and the double garage was full of cameras and tripods. The quiet, cream-painted house concealed a "madness" factory, where people trotted from room to room and from phone to phone. There were beds and couches everywhere, in hallways and on landings. When you stayed at Billy's you'd go down a corridor and meet a dozen people you didn't know: there'd be someone borrowing equipment, someone looking for a can of film, someone en route to catch a plane.

The house hopped and bumped and shouted twenty-four hours out of twenty-four. It was inhabited by secretaries, accountants, designers, scriptwriters and recordists. It was the audio-visual game in miniature and Fran organised it on her own.

A nurse brought in my breakfast and I sat up to get at it.

"The doctors say you'll be fine," said Fran; "I asked them. You can come out tomorrow."

"I'll come and pick you up," said Billy, "after the show." He came over and put a fresh bottle of gin by my bed. "There's lemonade too, and ice."

"Thanks." Suddenly I was lonely and terrified. It was one of those moments of cold panic when you remember that death is real. I wanted someone to load me gently into a warm and comfortable car and drive me away to my shack. The Bunce could be one of two things: it could be what Rosser said it was or it could be the guys who had done the Heathrow job. Whichever it was, Jim was dead and I didn't want to be next—slaughtered, nailed to a fence and left to rot like a dead weasel. I was all alone in a narrow bed with a world outside that was full of coppers who weren't coppers, and with crooks who carried roses round their automatics. I wasn't brave and I didn't want to die.

"Perhaps I should come anyway," I said, "there'll be something for me to do."

Fran would have guessed all of what I was thinking. She was a rarity, she thought about other people, felt for them. She came over, and took my hand and squeezed it.

"Don't be silly," she said, "they'll need you in Edinburgh. I'll have to be back in London by then, this is the best place to be." She bent down quickly and kissed me. She was so good, that woman.

"Drink the gin," said Billy, "and watch the tele. We'll come by tomorrow as soon as we're loaded." He gave me a fistful of twenty-pound notes. "Get anything you need." Fran put her hand into the hair at the back of my neck and shook my head gently, telling me, in secret, not to be scared. Then they both turned and, hand in hand, they walked briskly out, letting the door swing so violently that it made its peculiar noise several times.

At lunchtime the next day Duncan strode in and said we were on our way to Edinburgh; the Volvo and the van, a hired one to replace Panurge, were outside. I was dressed and packed and, within a minute or two, was standing in the car-park. Billy was leaning against his car and looking at the new truck.

"*Adieu*, Panurge," I said.

"Goodbye, Jim," said Duggie, as angry as ever, or angrier.

"The funeral's the day after tomorrow," said Duncan, "there's no show, we'll all be able to come down for it."

"That's nice," said Duggie, "bloody nice," and he spat towards my shoe.

Billy took me with him in the Volvo. "I phoned the Nottingham law," he said. "No news of Nasty, they said it was far too early yet. I also send Jonathan round to the local law with my statement . . . they are in fact considering a drunken driving charge against me but they haven't made up their minds yet. They were quite nice about it, but they told Jonathan that your story about a blue truck is moonshine. One of their cars was travelling right behind us . . . the van went straight off the road they said, and I was driving."

"Well, shit," I said, "it's not true, Billy."

"You know what this means, don't you?"

"It means that there is a Bunce."

"Yes, it means that, or it means that you are lying or crazy."

I lowered my head into my hands and massaged my scalp for a while, to get the blood to flow.

"Crazy," I said, "that's always possible."

CHAPTER FIFTEEN

The Funeral

It was a fine day for the funeral. We got up well before dawn in Edinburgh so that we could make Newcastle by nine o'clock. It was August but the air was sharp and even breakfast was wintry; porridge preceding kippers.

It was an unreal drive, everything seemed unreal that morning: the chill outside the car, a huge Billy Jay wreath overflowing on the roof-rack, Jim dead. The Volvo swooped along the empty roads, Billy driving slowly because there were no other cars to compete with. We passengers, hired mourners, clasped our knees and stared out of the windows and evaded talk. There was a hoar frost that morning and the light touch of it was heavy enough to make the countryside still, except for our flowered transport. I felt like a fugitive running into the country of the plague, with only a nosegay for protection.

The sunlight in the pale fields was green and slanted towards us at an odd angle. I gazed into it, looking for movement but there was none. One scene followed another like colour slides dropping from a carousel, falling away for ever. The cattle stood motionless, there wasn't a crow in the sky and the rookeries were dark in the dead elms. It was an exhausted landscape and nothing in it had courage enough to carry on.

The Funeral

We went to the strangest of funerals. Poor Jim. At the centre of it all were his parents, in borrowed black clothes. They walked in bewilderment under a smell of incense of mothball, and the odour made them seem spiritual, as if they'd journeyed from the other side to fetch their son, their only son, and it was the unaccustomed flesh they wore that made them move so awkwardly. They were thin and stood close together, moving together, linked. They held hands and arms, shifting their limbs all the time, exchanging comforting words. "Don't take on, Dad, don't take on, it does no good." "There, Mother, we'll be all right, have to be, we've got to get through it."

Jim's parents ran a grocer's in Greenford and I'd been there once. It was one of those places from everybody's childhood, running errands for pocket money. I could imagine it locked and barred that day, weak light squeezing round the shutters to touch the shelves, the cans of sardines gleaming. And the smells there too: ham, cheese, broken eggs, coffee, all mixed up.

We arrived in good time and found the parents standing by themselves in the middle of a lawn of remembrance, a lawn as bright as the water from a tin of peas and starched like a tablecloth, freshly ironed and expertly hemmed. Fran had sent them up from London in a hired Daimler and they'd stayed in a hotel; what had they talked about? They'd only gone on with the shop for Jim's sake, not that he would have wanted it but he could have sold it for the good-will, bought a house for himself when he married.

We got out of the car and walked over. Billy wore a fawn suit. He put his hands into his trouser pockets and pulled them out again. I didn't have suits any more, instead I had on a navy-blue sweater and brown jeans. Duncan carried a sports jacket over his arm. Duggie had a jeans jacket, Les Eastaugh a leather one. We weren't formal but we were clean.

When we got to Jim's parents we took a deep breath, ducked into their cloud of camphor, fumbled for their hands and shook them, telling them that Jim had been our mate and had made us laugh. It was a shame that we couldn't tell them *how* he'd made us laugh. They nodded and told us that it was nice of us to come and good of Billy to pay for everything like he had, and they touched their eyes and tried not to cry and turned away when they did.

Billy and I went back to the car and lifted the wreath down from the top of the aluminium roof-rack. We carried it between us and upended it on the lawn. It dwarfed the parents when they came towards it, and it was too big for them to do anything with. They turned, uncomfortably, and looked behind them, making us look round too. Beyond a gravelled walk, on another lawn, we saw an amazing spread of flowers and wreaths, sprays, bunches and crosses, staining the grass with colour. Most of them had Morley cards on and they were all Jim's.

On the far side of the flowers, across another raked path and on another compressed lawn stood a crowd, marshalled in rows, separate, not touching each other, in different lines at different angles, hardly moving.

The riggers were there, all of them; gypsies, their jeans pale and dirty, their leather jackets torn and marked with oil. They had their women with them too, dressed in soft robes like saris; their thighs shifted and gleamed underneath. The men showed stubble on their chins, the women had creases of sleep in their grubby faces. Someone out of sight at the back of the group touched quiet chords on a guitar and whiled away the time.

The Morley office was present in numbers, standing with the riggers but in a group apart, not talking, suited and buttoned and clean, both men and women. In front of them all stood Max, his round face still and solemn, his grey-streaked hair moving gently against his head in the slight breeze. He wore a dark suit and his black leather gloves looked stuffed with sand. He, together with everyone else, stared at Billy and me as we struggled with the giant wreath.

A loaded hearse, not the one we were waiting for, went by us on its way to the crematorium chapel. A car-load of

The Funeral

mourners followed and, as soon as it had passed, Billy and I moved away from Jim's parents, bearing the wreath between us, looking for a space amongst the other flowers.

There was none to be found. We stood our tribute up on end to begin with, but it was too tall and too heavy to remain upright on its tripod and it fell over. I rearranged the other wreaths, making room, piling crosses and hearts on top of one another. Billy stepped backwards onto the path, clasped his hands and looked down at the ground as if he were praying. Duncan and Duggie, Les and me did the same for a minute. When the minute was over Billy crossed the path to join Max; so did the others, except Duncan; he went back to Jim's parents and I followed him to listen.

"You mustn't think anything wrong about the way we're dressed," he said to Jim's father, "it doesn't mean any disrespect. You see, we live out of suitcases on these trips. Those fellas over there," he meant Kevin and the riggers, "they liked Jim a lot, he liked them. They probably drove all night to be here, you know what I mean?" The little man nodded and held onto his wife a little tighter.

As we waited, the tall brick chimney which rose above the crematorium shuddered and a fistful of brown smoke exploded out of the air and stood stiffly against the sky. Then, as I watched, the smoke faded without drifting and that part of the sky went grey. Jim's mum pushed her face into the shoulder of her husband's overcoat and cried. "There, there, Mother," he said, patting her like some old cat, "don't take on."

Duncan and I moved away to leave them alone and joined the others, waiting tranquilly on the lawn. Heads nodded at us, Kevin smiled and drew on his cigarette and Max watched the ceremony preceding ours. The corpse had gone into the chapel and the scattered bereaved followed it, looking at the ground.

At last Jim came. I don't know how we knew it was Jim, Fran had arranged the funeral. The man sitting next to Jim's driver knew who we were, but then he'd seen the body, the clothes.

The hearse came to a halt in front of Jim's parents, like it had been programmed to run out of petrol there. The driver sat where he was, the undertaker clicked open his door, slipped out and went straight to Jim's mum like an uncle.

The mourners from the previous funeral reappeared and walked away to where their cars were parked; they were talking now, glad that it was over. The close relatives wept and followed where they were led. An official came to the door of the chapel, nodded, and went back inside. Four men came to the back of Jim's hearse, rolled him out and hoisted the veneer box onto their shoulders, faces set, just another job at a fiver a time.

I thought of Jim's boots nudging about in the coffin, wondered if he had them on. We followed Jim and his parents into the chapel. There was piped organ music, low, undenominational, inoffensive. At the door I stopped with Kevin as he dropped his joint to the ground and trod on it. "I don't know why I bother," he said, "must be a lot more smoke inside than out."

Jim was put onto the conveyor belt in the open space in front of the pews. The music stopped and a clergyman in a white surplice, undenominational like the music, stood up and said he wasn't interested in who we were or what religion we followed but, if we had loved Jim and felt we should weep for him, then that's what we should do, all we could do.

Jim's mother broke down completely then, and her sobs filled the chapel. Jim's father patted her some more, but he had to lower his head and his sobs were soon to be heard with hers.

The clergyman went on with his prayers. Then came some more taped organ music and the maroon curtains on remote control began to close between Jim's box and ourselves. Jim's mother collapsed onto her seat and her husband followed, half holding her, half leaning against her. Once those curtains met in the middle there was no more Jim, no more little boy in cowboy boots to argue with, no more shirts to iron. One of the riggers' girls went forward in front of us all and sat by Jim's mum and cuddled her and wept with her, big gobs of tears.

The canned music came to an end and one of the riggers at the back took up a guitar and a girl sang. I don't think she'd meant to but she wanted to do something and it was all she could do. She sang slowly, a blues, and it was just as corny as the organ music, but it was alive and it helped. The clergyman moved forward and took Jim's mother by the hands and talked to her. The rest of us turned and went outside, where the next funeral party stood waiting, and beyond that the next, undertakers and relatives standing together alongside their hearses, spaced and orderly, waiting their turn.

We gathered into circles of people who knew each other. The riggers lit what might have been cigarettes and inhaled. I pushed through several groups to get to Billy and when I reached him I touched his sleeve; he turned and I nodded to where, just inside the gates, a police car was parked. The two policemen whose car it was were walking towards the riggers, moving slowly.

Billy stretched himself up on his toes and looked ready to bat the policemen into the ground, but he didn't have to. The riggers turned and walked round the edge of the crowd and went through the gates towards their two micro buses. The policemen changed direction to intercept, but Billy had moved quickly and put himself in their way. I didn't hear Billy's words when the coppers went to pass him but I saw his lips move. "Bugger off," he said.

As the coppers turned to give Billy their attention, Rosser's big black Ford drove into the gardens; it saw the policemen and braked and ducked its nose. Next to Rosser sat a driver, a square man with lumpy shoulders. He was a better driver than he looked. A word from Rosser and he threw the car into reverse, and without twisting in his seat he backed the Ford out into the wide gravelled road that led to the crematorium. It happened so quietly that only Billy, the policemen and myself were aware of it.

The coppers forgot Billy and dodged between the hearses, going back to their car. Before they reached it, Rosser's window had come down and he held out a briefcase, lengthways, squinting over the top of it. There was no noise but the two rear tyres of the police car subsided. Again, Billy saw it, the two policemen saw it and I saw it, but no one else did. Rosser's car was driven away.

Billy and I looked at each other at the very moment the two policemen looked at us to see if we'd seen; to them it appeared that we hadn't. One of them sat himself in the car and spoke into his radio, the other opened the boot and took out the jack.

Jim's parents were sitting on a wooden bench on the lawn of remembrance, looking at their son's flowers. In front of them, but unseen, passed the members of the Morley office, bending low, whispering condolences and goodbyes. Max took the father's hand in farewell and held it, while he said, "You can be proud of your son, he was doing important work with us, and doing it well. Nature will love him, be sure of that." Even then Max did not let go of the hand, but Jim's dad wouldn't look up and at last Max walked away to his car.

"We'd better say goodbye," said Duncan, "there's nothing we can do now."

We stood by the bench and eventually Jim's dad saw us. He got to his feet, his eyes red and his face grey with pain. He looked up at Billy, "Thank you for coming," he said, "Jim told me a lot about you boys, about all of you. Thank you, Mr. Jay, for everything, the car, the flowers, your wife was very kind, making all the arrangements, you must have spent a lot of money, I don't know how we'd have managed on our own, it was such a shock. You've all been very kind, all of you."

We wanted to leave but we stood there, waiting for him to say something else or go away. "It was the least we could do," said Billy, "we worked together, Jim was a friend."

There was another silence.

"Is there anything else?" Billy asked, bending his head, whispering as to an invalid.

"Yes," said Jim's dad. He took a fiver from his pocket and tried to give it to Billy, who shied away, putting his hands behind his back. "Don't get me wrong," said the little man, his face screwing up with anguish in case we did. "You must take it." He grabbed Billy's arm with all his puny strength and shoved the fiver into the limp hand at the end of it. "I know you fellas . . . you're bound to stop for a drink on the way back. I'd like you to have one on me, on Jim if you like, then; just for you four because he talked a lot about you, he liked every one of you. I'd come with you, like to I mean, but I've got to look after his mother, haven't I?" His voice faltered. "Look, just have a drink on the way back, that's all, just you Magic Lantern lot, all right? Goodbye, and ta."

He ducked his head and went over to his wife and sat beside her. Their Daimler driver stood nearby, twisting his cap impatiently in his hands. The next veneer box was carried into the chapel and Jim's undertaker said goodbye and began loading Jim's flowers into the empty hearse—to take to a local hospital, he said. The parents sat and watched until there were no flowers left and we watched with them. Then the brick chimney gave a shudder and we looked upwards and there was Jim, another stain on the sky, like a misdirected spit of tobacco juice on a dirty window pane.

DAYS 19–21

CHAPTER SIXTEEN
Edinburgh / Glasgow

Half way to Edinburgh we left the motorway and found a pub like Jim's dad had wanted us to. We sat round a formica-topped table and ordered some steak sandwiches and drank till the fiver was gone. I put some money in the juke-box and played what Jim would have played, and that was that.

The Edinburgh show gave us few problems; Les had taken Jim's place on lights and everything ticked over the same as before. Max had full confidence in us now and, between shows, flew to London, Paris or Brussels. He was a busy man, arranging the European tour.

"You'll come to Europe?" Billy asked.

"No," I said. "I'll stay to the end of this, back to the Stardust, the last show, that's all. I want to go home. There are plenty of stage-managers."

After the performance Kevin brought his gypsies in and struck the set. Kevin was always there but the faces of his gang changed all the time. "I don't know half of them," he said. "They hire themselves, fire themselves."

He disappeared in the middle of the night, taking Merrie Englande with him. Magic Lantern followed the next morning, destination Glasgow. When we got there, Hotel Cameronian, Jonathan Lane was lunching alone in the à la carte restaurant.

Billy had briefed Jonathan fully in Newcastle, telling him everything and sending him back to London to track down the Loss Adjustor in order to discover how to stake a claim in the reward. Jonathan was a sharp solicitor with a deep reserve of sly energy and very useful to Magic Lantern in many ways; he had contacts everywhere.

Billy and I sat down with him and ordered a meal and a couple of bottles of Bordeaux. There were two empty bottles of Lacombe on the table already but when the new wine came Jonathan poured himself a tumbler-full, ignoring us.

"There must be prohibition in London," said Billy, and poured me a glass, then one for himself.

"You're lucky," said Jonathan. "If you'd kept me waiting any longer I'd have been too pissed to talk."

Jonathan had long lank hair, dark grey, parted in the middle, and it fell down in flaps to his ears. He had a big nose, indistinct at the edges, and his eyes, too small, did their best to hide beneath his forehead. The muscles behind his lips were soft from frequent eating, good eating. Billy trusted him; I didn't but never thought it worth mentioning.

"I went to see the Loss Adjustor," Jonathan said, with his mouth full. "He's a very nice chap, auditing, insurance, that kind of thing. You'll be pretty lucky, he thought, twenty thousand."

"What do you mean?" said Billy, taking his glass away from his mouth. "Ten per cent of a million quid at least, that makes a hundred thousand, could be more. Don't you let me down, Jonathan . . . have you done a deal on the side?"

"That's a nasty idea," said Jonathan. He went very red but then he had drunk a lot of Bordeaux.

"The world is full of nasty ideas," answered Billy, "and only some of them are mine."

"I spent a lot of time with the Loss Adjustor," Jonathan went on. "He explained the whole business to me, took a lot of trouble, there are other claimants, with a better case than yours."

Billy swore and the whole dining-room rattled. Every head

turned towards us and then turned away. Billy looked at me and I said, "Just what Rosser said."

"I don't care," Billy wagged a finger at me, "nobody could have a stronger claim than mine. I was with those crooks all the way and nobody saw them but me, I was there. Did you find out who these other claimants were?"

"I tackled the Loss Adjustor about that. He said his evidence came from the police and they would not divulge the names of their witnesses, they have no legal obligation to and the Loss Adjustor doesn't need to know them anyway. It seems they are members of the criminal world themselves. If the police release their names then they are no longer useful as informers."

"The Bunce," said Billy.

Jonathan laughed. "Oh, I told the Loss Adjustor about that too; he thought it was a good story but he didn't believe a word of it. You don't believe a word of it yourself, Billy, you told me so. That man Rosser wants some of your money but there's no reason why you should give him a penny of it."

Billy took a mouthful of wine and shook his head as he swallowed. "I want you to go right back to this Loss Adjustor and I want you to tell him that I shall fight any decision that gives any of the reward to these police informers, up to the House of Lords, if necessary." Billy always mentioned the House of Lords when it came to legal matters. "And I want their names and details of the information they gave, and I want to meet them. Tell him I'll use the press, the media, the lot. I'm not lying down under this. He can't go throwing my money about—what's he think I am, a flag day?"

"It might cost you more than it's worth, but if that's what you want."

"That's what I want."

"He may react unfavourably."

"Let him. Did you get anything on Rosser?"

"Not really . . . friend of a friend of mine got into the records computer, there is a Rosser that might be your Rosser, he couldn't say. Used to be a copper, there were suspicions, nothing proved but he resigned from the force, subsequent convictions for robbery, present whereabouts unknown."

I thought of a question. "The Loss Adjustor, what's he like?"

"Nice enough, gentle manners, thorough, knows his job, quite helpful."

"Yeah, but what's he look like?" asked Billy, and closed his eyes to listen for the answer.

"He's a very big man, fat, except it's muscle, light on his feet—strange that. Sweats a bit, very polite. He has a photograph in a Woolworth's frame on his desk, wife and two daughters, look like primary-school teachers, standing outside a semi-detached; could be anywhere, Raynes Park."

He sent Jonathan home on the shuttle plane as soon as he'd finished his meal and his bottle. He didn't tell him that old Nasty and the Loss Adjustor were one and the same person. He thought Jonathan would work better if he didn't know.

"Keep ferreting," Billy said, as Jonathan was leaving. "Get onto Kelly at the *Daily Mirror*, see if he can find out anything about those informers, we must have their names. I want to pull them out into the open, there's a lot of money involved, Jonathan, and I want it."

In the conference room Billy and I took over from the others while they had lunch and we carried on knitting our wires into the set. Well fed, Duncan, Duggie and Les came back in the middle of the afternoon and we did a technical run-through, then another. Eventually, we rehearsed with Max and the Morley men and Max was happy.

"Great team, Billy," he said. "We'll run one full rehearsal tomorrow morning, just before the show; have dinner."

Then he swung off with his acolytes, up to one of his seminar rooms to plan Europe, an Eisenhower rolling up the continent like a carpet and taking it home over his shoulder as a souvenir.

It was another good dinner and we drank a lot of brandy;

an evening of relaxation, coming after the funeral. I must have been fairly far gone because I felt a surge of loyalty rise in me for Billy and his reward. Billy sometimes did this to me and it was difficult to explain how. I felt a sudden confidence in his capacity to take on anybody and win. I felt that if he stood firm long enough, the enemy would surrender and leave us alone. We could defend ourselves with publicity; after all, that was what we were supposed to be good at, that was our work. If Billy kept his nerve it would be all right, and I would stand by him, he was my friend.

Billy and I had adjoining rooms on the third floor of the Cameronian. Fairly late that evening we stood side by side, swaying, trying to get our keys into locks. I dropped mine and giggled.

"Goodnight, Mike," Billy said, and as he pushed his door a voice came from inside, "Come on in, Billy, I've been waiting for you."

With my tipsy bravery fresh in my mind, I went over to Billy only to have him step backwards onto my foot. I cursed and leant against the door-frame, twisting my head to look into Billy's room.

Rosser was lying on one of the beds, feet up, shoes off. The colour television was going and in his left hand he held a pint mug of gin and tonic. People always laughed at Billy Jay's drink but they soon adopted it, especially when Billy was buying the gin. In Rosser's right hand was his automatic. "Hello, Mike," he said, "come on in, both of you, have a drink."

I followed Billy into the room, my foot hurt. We sat down, Billy on a bed, me in an armchair and Rosser switched off the television. "That's a film I like," he said. In spite of his bullet head and greasy hair, Rosser was easy to be with. Amongst all the people who were running in and out of our lives during those days and nights, Rosser was somehow reassuring. If he was a con-man, he was a good one; if a crook, he had a sense of humour. Honest was too strong a word for him but he was straightforward.

"You didn't stay long at the funeral," said Billy.

"That's right," said Rosser, "I didn't. The Bunce know that I'm into this business, and they would like to put me away or persuade me to disappear, and they will if they catch up with me."

Billy got up and went to the wardrobe. Rosser watched him but Billy only brought out another bottle of gin.

"I wouldn't know how to shoot a gun if you stuffed one up my nostril," he said, and he went to the fridge in the corner for tonic and ice. "If the Bunce is all you say it is, they're bound to catch up with you, aren't they?"

"Yes, but it won't be quite so easy for them now. I've got a couple of hard men looking after me, all the time."

"I like you, Rosser," said Billy, "only I can't believe a word you say." He handed me a drink and my head moved like it had a universal joint under it.

"Okay, it sounds like a tall story, but it isn't."

From where I sat in my armchair I decided that I wasn't scared of Rosser any more. "How come," I said, my head jerking upwards, "you're so damn articulate?" I finished speaking and my head plunged downwards.

Rosser enjoyed the question, perhaps he'd been waiting for it.

"You mustn't imagine that all crooks are dummies, any more than all coppers are. Time is what you get in prison, correspondence courses and excellent conversation." Rosser laughed and remembered things he wasn't going to share with us. "I'm not asking you to believe much, you know. It's an accepted fact that some coppers cream a little off the top. I've seen it happen, so has everyone. There was that bank robbery a couple of years ago, St. James's Square, you remember, the big one? Enormous loot, the papers said. I was on that job, all we had time to take was eighty thousand. It was a good night's work, though, and we were well satisfied. When the bank counted up they said there was three hundred and fifty thousand pounds missing. Where did the rest go, I wonder? They reckoned the law was carrying evidence out of the vaults in big plastic bags. You know it happens, what you don't know is how organised it all is. And another thing, the Bunce often organises its own robberies, that way it has two options. It can peddle the proceeds in the normal way through one of its fences, or it can 'discover' and 'recover' the stolen property and claim the reward. A good reward is the best; the money gets laundered for them and the police get good publicity into the bargain. It's a nice business and, like all big business, it keeps quiet, most of the time . . . but if you push it hard enough the Bunce will smash you into the ground. It doesn't want to take you out, Billy, because of the coverage you got in the press, because you are noisy, but it will if it has to. A road accident is easy to arrange—well, you've had one of those, you don't need a drawing."

"If there's such a bloody risk, why are you taking it?"

I raised my head and it pulled me deep into the armchair and I stretched out, concentrating a little part of my brain, distant and sober, on what was being said.

"I don't have any option, I need the cash." Rosser settled back on the bed to explain. "I fixed up the Heathrow deal, right? I use the best men and they get the best money. Most of my share was spoken for, I've got some tied up abroad too, I'm short."

"And you want some of mine," said Billy sneering, "so that you can set up house in Brazil?"

"Not exactly. The four men I used on the last job were American, no form here; they flew in from the States and were meant to go straight back home afterwards. Those men are very well-connected, and they are often needed; now they are being missed. Two of their friends have come over especially to see me, to remind me of something that I hadn't forgotten."

"So?"

"I have a new job now. Those four men on remand have to come out of jail, before sentence . . . afterwards it becomes too difficult, separate jails, security wings, you know, not that I'd have any interest in it by that time."

Billy sat up on his bed, astounded. He drew a finger across his throat. "You mean . . . ?" He was loving it.

Rosser was quite touched. "It would be cleaner than a road accident. A bullet in the head over in Northern Ireland, just another corpse."

Billy swung his feet to the floor and took up the bottle of gin. "It's the Mafia, isn't it?" He sent me a look which said, "I told you so." I fed the information into a cubicle of my mind and hoped I'd find it there when I woke up.

"Don't jump to conclusions, Billy." I liked the way Rosser didn't use the Mafia to impress us. It made me wonder.

Billy wondered too and the idea of putting one over on Nasty appealed to him. "All right, if the Bunce is as strong as you say it is, how do you protect me and get my money?"

"I can't guarantee a thing, not many people take on the Bunce and get away with it. I only have one advantage, I can move in their territory, I know how they work. On top of that, I have a little organisation of my own. It's not as good as the Bunce, I don't have access to the tax-payer's money, but there are certain people I can call on."

"How do you know so much about the Bunce?" I asked. "Do they publish a year book?" I get witty when I'm drunk.

Rosser lost his composure and I thought I'd caught him. He looked at me hard.

"Because," he said, "I once ran a section for it. I'm the worst thing there is—a renegade renegade. The man you call Nasty would like to see me in hell. When I left the Bunce a few years ago I took some of their money with me. If I stay in England they'll get me all right. I was on my way out of the country, the Heathrow job was to set me up."

There was a long silence after that. I wasn't far from sleep.

At last Billy said, "And you say there's nothing I can do on my own?"

"Well, your man Jonathan can fight for a while, but sooner or later they'll have him by the short and curlies. The police don't have to disclose their sources of information—the insurance companies don't have to say where the money goes, it's a closed shop."

I held my chin in my hand to keep my head straight. "If Nasty has got it wrapped, why has he put so much effort into Billy? Answer that."

"Nasty has a lot of power," said Rosser, "touch him in his pride and you switch on all the power he's got. Billy, because he's Billy," Rosser raised his glass, "made something simple into something difficult. Billy got publicity. Nasty came to see Billy because he wanted to settle things quietly, to warn him that things weren't what they seemed. Billy made trouble and Nasty decided that there were other ways to make Billy agreeable."

"What would have happened if Billy hadn't been greedy, had gone along with it?"

"What's greedy about it?" said Billy, "It's my bloody money."

"Using a front man to carve up a reward is fairly common practice, but it's always tricky when outsiders are involved. Nasty would have preferred to have done a quick deal with Billy. He would have said, as a Loss Adjustor, there can be more than one, that it was his duty to point out that the deliberations over the money could drag on for years, that there were other strong claims in for the reward money, in other words, settle quickly and get something for certain. If Billy had agreed, and most people would have, he'd have got a cheque for as little as Nasty thought he could get away with, twenty, fifteen, ten grand. When the noise had died down, the balance, anything between eighty and a hundred and twenty thousand, say, would have been paid over to Mr. X and Mr. Y, very quietly; and then, just as quietly, they would have invested it in Vauxhall Insurance, for example, and the money would have been as safe and as honest as Princess Margaret's."

"Well, I'm buggered," said Billy, "there's no answer to that."

"Where does Nasty come from?" I asked.

"Nowhere. He spent years as an accountant, then there was a time when nobody knew where he was. He came into contact with the Bunce through working on fraud cases. He's a magician with figures. He was put under surveillance and then the Bunce signed him up, gave him a lot of work. He was meticulous, reliable, expert, small-minded, and up the ladder he went. Best of all, he has no form and never will have now, as clean as the Commissioner, he is, just an insurance man."

"Is a Bunce man always employed as the Loss Adjustor?"

"By no means; Nasty is Vauxhall Insurance, he was just asked to do the job, it was just the luck."

"So what happens when the Loss Adjustor is straight?"

"Makes no difference, does it? They can only pay out on police information, they have to make their decisions on that, so it goes."

I got out of my armchair and stretched full-length on the floor.

"What's to stop me," said Billy, truculent, "going to people I know in the press and blowing the thing wide open?"

Rosser laughed and it was like galvanised nails rattling in a tin. "Nothing, but you know how things are done. There's a lot of money involved and journalists and the rest of them are all as vulnerable as you are. The press is tied into the status quo and the status quo loves a copper. You might make some headway because you haven't got any form, but they'd soon find you some. You'd be easy, drunken driving, resisting an officer, drunk and disorderly, receiving stolen property. You wouldn't look too good after a while."

I heard Billy lean over the space between the two beds and empty the bottle into the glasses. He didn't offer me any and I shoved my head into the carpet to stop it moving.

"How can you expect to protect me, then?"

"I can't answer that, Billy, I'll have to see."

Billy got up from his bed. I opened an eye and watched his feet move towards the window; he stared through the double-glazing, looking into the dark well that was outside. He was trying to decide.

"I'm no straighter than anyone else," he said. "Like most people, I've stolen the odd this and that, bought stuff that fell off lorries, nicked things when I was a kid—and even now; petrol of course, ashtrays from hotels, but that's not in your class, is it? Stealing doesn't worry you?"

"It worries me if I get caught," said Rosser, "otherwise not a bit, why should it? Kruger rands, bullion, jewellery, it's fat cash being shifted from one account to another, a lot of figures adding noughts, Monopoly money; what rich men keep in wall-safes to make them think they've got big cocks. That kind of money's mine if I can get it, it's only theirs as long as they can hang onto it, it's a free country."

I opened my eyes again. Billy had turned to lean against the window-sill. He would agree with Rosser on that score. Billy would have sailed with Henry Morgan.

"Not one touch of the Robin Hood's?" he asked. Behind him the dawn dropped down into the hotel's centre.

"I like to steal from the rich," said Rosser, "mainly because they're the ones with the money, not much sense tunnelling into Peabody Buildings, is there? And the poor I give to is me and mine."

Billy came and sat in the armchair I had left and put his face between his hands. I rolled over and, on my hands and knees, went to the bathroom to pee. I felt ill.

"You're saying," said Billy, "that if I don't come in with you I don't stand a chance?"

"Yes," said Rosser. "And if I don't have the use of some real cash very soon, to get those four Americans out of jail, then the other two downstairs will see to it that I die."

Silence. They sat there listening to my piss clatter on the water. I finished, went back into the room and stretched out on the bed that Billy had vacated.

"Fifty-fifty," said Billy, "whatever it is?"

"Yes," said Rosser, "fifty-fifty."

"I'm a witness," I said, and rolled onto my side.

"He's pissed," said Billy. "All right, Rosser. You can manage my interest for a half share."

Rosser looked pleased. "That's good, Billy, now I can move."

"What would you have done," my head was speaking from the other side of the room, "if Billy had said 'no'?"

Rosser sat on the edge of the bed and pulled his shoes on, did up the laces, took his gun and slipped it under his arm. "I wouldn't have done anything," he said, "it's the two men downstairs. They're not kinky like Nasty, they'd have a bullet into the back of Billy's neck."

Billy paled. "Those damned Americans," he said, "they don't care what they are, as long as they're thorough."

It was about then that I passed out.

DAYS 22–26

CHAPTER SEVENTEEN

The Picnic

The Morley presentations were going admirably. The Glasgow show went without a hitch and we moved along to Carlisle and did one there, Day 25. That was fine too. The Morley Pioneers were working hard, recruits came in from all over the country to learn how to see life in the Morley way, and Max said that Magic Lantern was the best, the only audio-visual company in the world. His smile got bigger and more sincere.

One evening, it was about three days after seing Rosser, I was sitting in the foyer of the Carlisle Hotel and drinking with Billy. The others had gone out to find a restaurant for a change, and to drink the local beer. Billy and I were talking about the reward; but then we hardly talked about anything else. We kept spinning the facts round and round, pulling the levers, pushing the buttons, hoping that the truth would come up like three cherries on a fruit machine. We lost our bet every time.

As we talked the phone rang, it was on the coffee table to Billy's right. Whenever Billy walked by a phone it rang, and it was always for him. We'd been on location in Wales once, filming in a tiny village street. About ten yards from us was a red phone-box, which rang while we were working, and we laughed and said it was bound to be for Billy. I picked up the receiver because I was nearest and said something in stage Welsh: "Mount Snowdon brothel 'ere, boyo,' that sort of thing. The voice on the other end said, "Stop screwing about and put Billy on." It was only Fran but it was uncanny. So when the phone rang, in the evening of Day 24, Billy picked it up automatically, barely bothering to interrupt what he was saying to me. The call was for him and he knew it.

I watched his face as he listened and something happened to it in a few seconds. The confidence left his skin. He put the receiver down and it looked like his eyes had been taken out with an ice-cream scoop; a silly old man's smile fumbled for his mouth.

"That was Jonathan," he said. "He knows who those police informers were." He had to moisten his throat to get the words out. "The Loss Adjustor just phoned him, very angry, something's happened . . ."

I nodded.

"Mr. X and Mr. Y . . ."

"Yes."

"They're dead, murdered."

I said nothing.

"According to Jonathan, the Loss Adjustor, Nasty, went berserk. You see, there's no one else to pay the reward to now, except me."

"How?"

"They were both shot in the back of the neck, at pub turning out time; one in Peckham, one in Brixton. They were both a bit drunk, going home alone. Someone walked up behind them, silencer, pumped a shot into them and kept walking."

"My God," I said, "Rosser."

"It's Mafia work," said Billy darkly, "what the hell are we into?"

We looked at each other, frightened.

"We're into trouble, Billy," I said. I'd never seen him look that scared before; death felt very close and all around in that hotel, and I felt suddenly that maybe our behaviour had been stupidly inappropriate all along; like tourists sniggering in the catacombs.

"You could be very rich and very dead in a day or two," I said.

Billy pushed his hand through his hair. "Well, Christ," he said, "some people manage to be alive and wealthy. I'm not asking much, some bastards drop into it the moment they're born."

"So you're envious, big deal."

"There's nothing wrong with envy," said Billy, "it's only another word for ambition." Occasionally a thought bolted out of Billy like that; a sparrow from a hole in the wall. It surprised and startled you and then it flew away.

After Carlisle, only Liverpool and Heathrow were left on the Morley schedule. It was nearly over and congratulations were due from Freddie Beckenbauer in New York. It now seemed certain that Magic Lantern would be asked to manage the European tour. It meant a lot of work for Billy but, by the time it was over, he would have cleared his overdraft. Billy had plans for expansion too, I didn't know what those plans were, nor did I want to know. I just knew that whatever he did would make little difference; within a year or two Magic Lantern would be back in the red. "That," as Billy always said, "was show business."

But he hardly spoke of the future during those last few days of the tour, he was preoccupied with thoughts of the reward, of Nasty and of Rosser. He was still convinced that he needed big money to be free and the work and the worry of it was wearing him down, but there was more. Mr. X and Mr. Y had gone and Billy was the only claimant. He felt threatened, insecure, and he looked it. Max and the Morley shows, the drink, the miles of motorway, the late hours, it had all rubbed against Billy, chafed his skin and left him tender, and nothing made him more desperate than the idea that the Bunce or Rosser might take his money away. The reward was his escape route, his short cut, and he clung to the thought even when it was obvious, it was to me, that Billy would never have the time to escape and would always hurtle straight past his short cut because he travelled too speedily. He was very much involved in the forward planning for the Morley trip into Europe, I knew that, but if it hadn't been Morley it would have been something similar. Billy was besieged but too busy to defend himself or to run away, even; he was always besieged, always busy. "Profit is a function of time," he quoted at me, day in, day out, but he never asked himself whose time and how much of it he had to give over, he just squandered it, sacrificing his life to work.

A trip like the Morley trip does that to everyone. We were cut off from anything real, at the same time we were sustained by Morley goods and Morley achievement. Morley men and women were with us every mile of the way and every day of the week. They looked to us for work and loyalty and in return they gave us the things we wanted. We knew them and they knew us but they knew more; they knew in advance our thoughts and desires.

It was true that they were going nowhere without Magic Lantern but Magic Lantern was only there, only existed in a sense, because Morley had put down the money. Max could replace us at any time and the thought kept him and his followers content. They ate, drank and sang Morley—and their songs were the worst; snappy American tunes, so cheerful, and we didn't have "Diver" Jim any more to put good vulgar words to them.

On Day 26 we moved from Carlisle to Liverpool, and on the road the motorway blues overtook us.

"You're driving like a moron," Duggie said.

It was true. Since the crash at Newcastle I spent more time looking into the rear-view mirror than at the road ahead. Duncan wasn't happy either.

"Let someone else drive," he said, "before I have to change my knickers."

Billy, randy for secrecy, had told Duncan and Duggie nothing about Rosser. All they knew was that a large blue lorry had forced us off the road through sheer bad driving. They had made no connection between the accident and the men dressed as policemen who had stopped Panurge on its way to Newcastle; they, Duncan was now convinced, had been members of the Heathrow gang.

I went along with the deception. If Duncan got too worried he might quit and Duggie would go with him; if we let Max down Billy would lose the European contract. The British tour was nearly over so what did it matter—Billy said —what Duncan and Duggie believed.

I flashed my headlights and the Volvo, driving in front, pulled over onto the hard shoulder. I pulled in behind it. We had decided to keep together on the motorway. If there was another accident we wanted witnesses.

The five of us, Les was travelling with Billy, leant against the car and raised our faces to the sun. We smoked cigarettes and took swigs from Billy's bottle. I felt the Volvo move in my back whenever a truck passed. We talked a little and at last decided to leave the motorway for an hour or so and look for a place to picnic. It was the day that decided us, really; a good warm day, only there on the road it smelt of diesel dust. Somewhere away from the traffic the air would be quiet and still, poised, not broken and smashed by passing juggernauts.

We stopped off in Kendal for supplies and Billy bought it all. We walked the length of the high street and we went into every grocer's and off-licence in the place. We had everything, fine bread, cold chickens, pineapple, bananas, slices of ham, pickled onions, grapes, custard pies, Pont l'Eveque, melons, burgundy, Bordeaux and cognac.

"Jesus," said Duggie, "how will we manage without the Food Supplement?"

Kendal was a good town. It was the holiday season and the place was crowded: men in shirt sleeves and girls in shorts, babies in pushchairs, their mouths stained, sucking lollies. The experience felt brand-new, walking in an ordinary street amongst ordinary people; it was alien after all the dark interiors of those concrete hotels. We were a handful of men on

The Picnic

their own, playing truant—certainly Billy and I were. We drank from our bottles and laughed across the whole width of the pavement, inviting every woman we saw to join us, but they just smiled and turned their heads away and their men looked stern.

At the end of the street by the car-park we stopped laughing. On the corner stood a policeman, I couldn't tell what rank he was; flat cap, blue shirt, with sleeves rolled right tight to the shoulders. Duncan and Duggie and Les raised their bottles and hooted a hello across the road at him. He didn't laugh but jerked his head in warning, meaning, "Don't you stay long on my manor, chummy." His hands were clasped behind his back and he rose and fell on his toes in the classic music-hall fashion. He did it on purpose.

"Who ordered a copper from Central Casting?" said Les. Wherever the policeman came from, he spent all his time watching Billy; watched him as we crossed the street, watched him as we drove away.

We left Kendal and headed west, towards Windermere and beyond, not looking at signposts. Duncan drove on, following roads that took his fancy; Billy came behind in the car. The narrow lanes twisted between the walls of dry stone. Wonderful country; green hillsides with a sheen of purple grass in the darker hollows, the walls fitting tightly into the rolling contours, up and down and out of sight.

Without a word, and quite suddenly, just when he felt like it, Duncan parked. We were on top of a steep hill and the walls were too high to see over. The road had broadened and there was space to park a car on each side, right on the brow. Part of the wall to our left had crumbled, there was a way into a field. Through the gap was a rocky platform, turfed over. A stream came from under the road, crossed the platform and fell from the edge of it, down into a steep-sided valley, dotted with large chunks of black stone which stood up energetically from under the grass. It was a turf as soft and as unified as any rubber-backed hotel floor covering. Here and there on its surface were spread clusters of sheep droppings looking like lumpy brown mushrooms. The stream was ice cold and we sank our bottles into it, as good as a fridge. On the hillside opposite a few unperturbed sheep raised their heads to stare at us, then went back to nibbling the carpet, keeping it tidy. We carried our provisions through and sprawled on the grass. I watched Billy and gradually the mortgages slipped from him and he relaxed. It was a perfect spot; no one knew where we were, no Max, no Rosser, no Nasty.

We began on the food, tearing at it with our hands, carving it into chunks, and soon we had greasy mouths and red wine on our teeth. The sheep got used to us and moved closer. Slowly the food disappeared, the ham, the cheese, the fruits; we were in no hurry and the next show was a long way away.

From time to time one of us went to fetch a bottle from the stream. The sun lowered itself steadily down the sky like a spider, the horizon receded and the fields rolled away to meet it, mile upon mile, as far as the sea. The valley altered shape, gently, lit by a colour-wheel revolving on a spotlight: grey, green, mauve, blue in the shadows, black under the rocks; the stream, mother of pearl. It was all silent and for an hour England was wide and spacious, and ours.

When we'd eaten we dozed and stretched, pulled our shirts off and sunbathed. Every now and then Les rolled over and said to the sky, "This is the life," and just as often Duggie answered with, "It better be."

"I couldn't stand it for long," said Billy, "I'd have to be doing something."

That was the trouble, he always had to be doing something and it was impossible to get out of his way when he did it. Staying away from him was no protection, cultivate your own garden and Billy would tramp all over it. He always found out where you lived. How many times had I answered a knock at home to find Billy on the doorstep, and behind him a girl's pale face looking out from the dark of a car window?

As we sat there in the Lake District, the shadows deepened, the sun's light turned cool and we put our shirts back on. The sheep looked at us anxiously, as our laughter rang down the valley, but we laughed even more and drank from the bottles.

We were still laughing when the two policemen came through the gap in the wall with the guns in their hands. Billy and I saw them first and we knew, we thought, who'd sent them. The others were still laughing, but gradually the laughter died and the sheep looked away. We kept still, all of us, and said nothing; caught on the ground no one tried to rise. The policemen stood one on either side of the gap, feet wide apart, tense, motionless, handsome, like heroes of the screen; so much so that I could hardly believe it when one of them gestured with his gun and said, "Okay, get your hands up, all of you." It was difficult to do what he asked, lying on the ground, but we did it.

When they were ready they told Billy to get to his feet, then me. One of them walked over to Billy and shoved his gun into the big confident gut and I saw the flesh shrivel up round the barrel. The copper placed his feet carefully when he moved and held his left hand in his tunic pocket, protecting something. "Turn round and walk down to the stream," he said, and Billy turned and walked. I set my weight onto one hip. I was frightened and my mouth was dry. I looked at the other three on the ground. The dull light of evening was rising from the horizon and their faces stood out from the dark grass like scattered white stones, round and pitted.

Billy walked down the narrow path to the stream below, stopping when he reached the tiny flat patch of pasture near where we'd submerged our bottles of wine. The policeman followed, treading carefully still, left hand in pocket. He ordered Billy to kneel and Billy, after only a moment's hesitation, did so. Before I had time to be scared for Billy I was scared for myself. The man turned and gestured to me; "Come down here, you," he said. I went down and the others sat up to watch, their hands clasped on their heads.

I got nearer to the man with the gun and I knew I was going to do anything he told me to. The sun was going down fast now and I looked at it. When I reached the stream the man said, "Do what I say or I'll put a bullet in your stomach; it hurts."

"Yes," I said, and waited while he took a woollen scarf from his neck.

"Blindfold him," the policeman said, and gave me the scarf.

My hands trembled. I moved nearer to Billy, he raised his head. His eyelids were screwed together and he was biting his lips so as not to make a sound, as if it mattered. I put the scarf around his head and tied it as tightly as I could.

"You bastard," someone shouted. It was Duggie and he meant me. He had got to his knees and would have climbed to his feet but he was clubbed down by the other policeman and he curled up in a tight ball like a woodlouse and held his head. My policeman sent me back up the path to the others and when I got there I looked at no one and sat as they were sitting, with my hands on my head. Duggie was not unconscious but blood poured from the side of his head.

Below us the policeman had placed the barrel of his gun at the back of Billy's neck. Billy recoiled from it and nearly fell. I heard the policeman's voice: "Killing those men in London was a mistake," he said, "now you're going out the same way."

"It wasn't me," Billy twisted his head. He was shouting. "I've been with the show, all the time, ask the boys. It was Rosser. Mike, tell them it was Rosser, for Christ's sake."

I found a voice, a dried up screechy thing. "It was Rosser, it was Rosser, leave Billy alone."

"It makes no difference," said the policeman, "we've topped Rosser already."

"It was Rosser, it was Rosser." I shouted it into the valley. The sheep ran a few steps then stopped. The policeman down below ignored me. I saw him bring his left hand from his pocket but I could not see what it held. With his right hand he levelled the pistol and fired a shot into the stream and all the sheep scurried away together. At the same time he brought his left hand down onto Billy's forehead, opening it

The Picnic

at the moment of contact. There was a sharp crack and the egg smashed and its yellow and white insides ran down Billy's face. The copper laughed and pushed Billy with his foot, hard, so that he rolled into the stream. I heard Billy take in a deep breath and he sobbed. The policeman turned and walked up the slope towards us, laughing, his right hand hanging by his side, holding the gun. The policeman behind me chuckled too, well amused.

For the first time in my life I really hated someone; and I hated myself too for being weak and cowardly, untrained and unprepared. Duggie had more courage in him than me, or the rest of us. He shouted and swore at the top of his voice, and he carried on with it until he was kicked twice in the side, and left breathless.

Then from the stream came a roar of anger, a giant's, perfect for that darkening valley. I raised my head. Billy's policeman was half way back to us and behind him was Billy, risen from the water, his clothes soaked and dripping, broken eggshell in his hair, gobbets of yolk on his face.

I've often seen Billy get angry on the road. I've seen him threaten hotel managers, I have seen him lift people from the floor and squeeze the damp out of their brains but I have never seen him so transfigured by rage and shame; his face was sublime, crazy.

He got to the copper in a bound, before the man had time to turn or lift the gun. Nothing could have stopped Billy, not even a bullet in the heart. The copper disappeared under Billy like a child under a falling factory wall and Billy's huge hands came down and the policeman screamed once and then was quiet but Billy kept punching and yelling and punching.

The second copper ran towards the edge of the valley waving his automatic. As he ran through us, Duggie caught the man's foot in his hand and pulled him over and we were all up and onto him and the hatred spilled out of us and we hit him. Duggie had a small rock in his hand and he brought it down on the copper's head. He raised it again but Duncan was behind him and snatched the stone and threw it away.

"Enough," he said. Duggie would not have accepted that from anyone else, but he and Duncan had grown up in the same street. Duggie was a tough boy with hard edges and he wanted to go on, but he took a deep breath and smiled. So did I, so did Les.

Billy was kneeling over his victim like a dog over a dead rabbit, his head hanging. We went down and pulled him to his feet and wiped away the egg, using the scarf, moist from the water. He staggered, his hands were bloody and his face was a ruin. While we helped him up the slope and through the hole in the wall, Duggie collected the guns and pitched them into the stream, and we left the policemen lying amongst the litter of our picnic: the bottles, the carcasses of chicken, the apple cores, the banana skins. I remembered the full litre of brandy and picked it up as we went.

We hoisted Billy into the passenger seat of the Volvo and strapped him in. He slumped against the door and stared with empty eyes through the windscreen.

"I'll drive the car," I said. I don't know why, my hands were as unsteady as anyone else's. I passed the bottle round and the four of us, standing in the road, took good long pulls at the brandy. "You three bring the van, we'd better keep together."

We found that we were staring at the police car parked on the brow of the hill and facing the opposite way to our vehicles. It was a smart car, pale blue, Rover 3500, the new luxury model. We looked at each other and went up to it and gazed down the long straight hill, into a painted landscape. Streaks of evening mist made the valleys seem flooded. Inside the police car a radio was arguing with itself. I couldn't understand the crackles, the codes.

Duggie went over to our van and came back with a bottle of meths and a newspaper. He emptied the bottle on the seats and then dropped it on the floor. I released the handbrake and we pushed the Rover to the middle of the road, holding it back on the brink of the hill. Duggie lit the newspaper with his Zippo, threw the flame into the car and we let go.

The Picnic

The Rover didn't leave the road until the very bottom of the long slope. It hit the stone wall on the left first, bounced up and over to the right, rebounded, rose over a hump, twisted onto its side, scraped along, turned and then demolished a stone wall, bursting into flames.

"The end," said Duggie, "to a perfect day."

We passed the cognac round and moved to the Volvo.

"What they never say about violence," said Duncan, his eyes brilliant, "is that it really is very satisfying."

DAYS 27, 28

CHAPTER EIGHTEEN

Liverpool

Billy sat next to me and stared at the lights on the road. I felt in the glove compartment, found some tranquillizers and pushed them into him. After that he held onto the cognac and sipped it while I drove. By the time we'd reached the hotel on the motorway south of Liverpool he'd emptied the bottle. The hotel was called The Fiesta.

The arm of the motorway led into the car-park, this time a plateau in front of the main doorway. To the side was a smaller entrance for baggage. I stopped the car there and the van went past me, going on to park by the big doors of the conference room at the back. In the yellow lights that shone down from the concrete canopy I could see that Billy was unconscious, his mouth open and his chin wet. His hair was a wadge of ochre, his eye sockets were as big as tennis balls.

I got out of the Volvo and walked towards the glass frontage. I raised my hand to push but the two panels slid back from me and I dropped my arm: damn doors were automatic. The porters inside smiled at each other.

"I'd like a wheel-chair," I said. "My boss has had a bad day and is under sedation." They looked at me then turned away. There were mirrors on the wall and I took a sideways glance; I had blood on my shirt and it was open to the waist. My thin hair stood up like a halo of madness; wine and grass had stained my jeans and my shoes were muddy. What my eyes looked like I couldn't tell, but my voice strained away from me when I spoke. "We've had a terrible day."

It was no good. "Everyone has to pass through reception first," said the senior of the two porters, straightening his back. "They'll have to tell us about the wheel-chair, not you."

"I don't want to take him through reception," I said.

"I can't help that," said the porter lifting his nose a degree, "you'll have to, it's more than my job's worth."

There was one in every hotel and that's what we called him, George Jobsworth.

The three others had parked the van and were standing behind me now. "It's George," I said, "he won't get the wheel-chair."

Duggie dropped his tool-box deliberately and took out a screwdriver, it had been sharpened. He pushed past me.

"Screw your job," he said, "you get the wheel-chair like he said or I'll put you in one." He stuck his screwdriver under the man's nose. The others looked as wild as me and the porter did as he was told. His colleague stood behind the counter and licked his lips. He had an alarm bell in front of him but he didn't press it.

Les was the cleanest of us and he went through to reception for our room numbers. We had to wait awhile for the chair but it came, and we eased the dead weight of Billy into it and wheeled him to the lift.

We crowded into Billy's room and the luggage followed along on a flat truck, the porters pushing it between them. Duggie gave them a quid each and they smiled and left. The room was maroon this time. "It's good to be home," said Duggie, "amongst the things you know and love."

It took the four of us to heave Billy onto his bed and to make him comfortable. We put a bottle of gin and some tonics on the table, covered him up and left him to sleep, then we bathed, changed our clothes and went down to the conference room where the set was waiting for us. One or two Morley people were working at bare wooden tables, but the main pressure, Max, was in Brussels. Billy could sleep for twenty-four hours if he had to.

During dinner I told the others what Billy and I thought was going on. It seemed only fair after the picnic. I told them nothing definite because I had nothing definite to tell them, I could only outline the options. Either Rosser was telling the truth or he wasn't; either Nasty and he were working together or they weren't.

They all took it pretty well; Duncan had toughened since the picnic. "And anyway," he said, "there's only two more shows to go."

First thing in the morning I went to see Billy but he was still sleeping. I thought about phoning Fran but then decided it was best not to worry her. Billy slept on and I went to morning rehearsals and ran everything through—the tapes, the speeches, the slides.

Billy came back to life at lunchtime and stood watching the screens as we checked one of the Morley stories. He was bathed, shaved and dressed in clean clothes. Apart from the soft creases of lavender under his eyes he appeared recovered, but he wasn't. His attack on the policeman had been magnificent but it had used him up. He nodded, he spoke, but there was no energy left. It wasn't Billy any more.

"Give in," I said to him when we were alone, "give in before they make you, it's not worth it. They'll get you one way or the other." But Billy just looked at the floor and shook his head.

Max flew in from Brussels, his men tagging behind him. We did a rehearsal and he was satisfied with it. Max noticed nothing different about us, did not remark on our silences or our fear; he was too full of his trip and what he was going to do in Germany, France, and Holland. It was a relief when the show came round that evening but, standing in the dark on the balcony with Billy, I wished it were all over; I wanted to go home.

"Billy," I said, "you don't really need me for the last show, someone else could do it."

"You can't walk out on me, not right at the end you can't."

"I've had enough, I'm scared. They haven't finished with us yet."

"I think they have," said Billy. "I've been thinking a lot today and I'm sure the worst is over. They can't do anything else, I'm the only one who can claim the reward, they'll have to do a deal with me, and on my terms. I'll say fifty-fifty, like with Rosser, it's the same."

"Do you think they killed Rosser?"

"Yes." Billy's eyes were anxious. "I do, but they can't kill me. I want the money, Mike, I want to get out of this business. I've got to move on."

Billy crossed to his console and flicked up a switch and the Morley introduction music began. I followed him.

"I don't care what happens, I'll keep going," he said.

"That's your trouble . . . it's not always a good thing."

"I'm only asking you to do the last lousy show."

"I'm really scared, Billy."

"Stay with me until the Stardust show and I'll give you a thousand out of the reward, on top of your wages."

"A thousand," I said, "a thousand?"

"Yeah, a thousand, you'll be able to stay in your shack for a year, maybe more, that should please you."

I didn't have to think about it. I was frightened but I wasn't frightened a thousand pounds' worth. "Okay," I said. "It's a deal."

Once he'd bribed me to stay Billy seemed less worried. I don't know what difference it made to him, maybe it was just the feeling of not being alone against whoever it was. At the very least I was someone to talk to.

After the show we went to dinner while Kevin and the riggers struck the set. It was late and we sat in a corner of the restaurant, watching everyone who came in. We were quiet, backs to the wall and wary, like old gunfighters.

When the meal was over the others went upstairs to try the gin in Billy's room. I made an excuse and said I'd follow on later. Billy wasn't happy at leaving me alone and argued against it but I needed to be away from him. I was excited by the idea of having enough money to give a whole year of my life to myself; not to work, to do what I wanted. I wasn't a bit worried about taking so much money from Billy, that was easy.

I went to the hotel bar. I ordered a gin and tonic of ordinary size and sat down in a corner to face the door. I wasn't alone for long. With a rustle of dress and leg a woman sat in the armchair opposite me. All the room in the world, I thought, and she has to sit here. There was a chuckle in a voice I'd forgotten, but remembered as I looked up, and there was Casey Roberts, sitting, legs crossed, laughing and leaning forward, beautiful and beyond my reach. Over her shoulder I could see the astonished face of the man she'd abandoned.

"Hello, Mike," she said.

"Casey, what are you doing here?"

"I'm working, a man to interview."

"Would you like a drink?" She shook her head and raised her right hand to show that she already had one, bought by the other man. She looked into me to see what I was thinking; no change. She was dressed in a soft fawn material, falling from her shoulders, designed for her; in it she was unconfined, behind the dress and not wearing it. That piece of cloth had cost a great deal of money. She smiled, letting me see that she remembered the things I'd said when I'd seen her the last time. I stared at my drink.

"Billy got his reward yet?"

I shook my head, hesitated, then decided that there was no point in telling her the story. "No, it's not been straightforward."

"Money never is," she said. She twisted her head and glanced at the man behind her; not to reassure him but with a whimsical surprise at still seeing him there.

"Who's that?" I asked.

"Nobody, he'll go soon."

My room-key lay on the table by my drink, it was attached

to a wide slab of plastic that bore its number. She pushed it round with her finger so that she could read it, 4823. She opened her eyes at me, like I was twelve and she was fifteen and taking me into the bushes for the first time. It was a bit like that, anyway.

"Why don't you go upstairs," she said, "and run me a bath?"

I held out my hand for her key. "Not in my room," she said, "the phone will be ringing all night. In yours."

At a party once I'd met a girl called Clare who'd picked me up and taken me home. She must have mistaken me for someone else in the dark. It was dark at the party, dark in the taxi and we'd had no coins for the light meter in her flat. She'd looked very surprised in the morning when she'd seen my face at last. I didn't complain. It is her body that I find beneath my fingers every time I dream myself awake. I remember her with her hair curling round her head and her breath as wholesome as witch-hazel. She'd stared at me in the morning; frank eyes with nothing to be got out of them. She'd got up, naked, and brought me coffee in bed and waited while I drank it, untroubled, saying nothing until I had finished, then she'd said I could go. Six o'clock on a Sunday morning and I'd walked southwards alone across an empty Hyde Park and looked about me. Everything was changed; now I didn't understand a thing.

I have never forgotten Clare and I have never seen her again. I have told no one about her but I think of her every day. It was she who had convinced me at last that there was a league in which I shouldn't play. It was with Clare that, for the first time, I had met that special texture of the flesh that comes from the mind, a muscular glee, an ironic sense of disdain behind the physical enjoyment. I had been twenty then, ten years later I met it for the second time in Casey Roberts. Warm from her bath she slid into my bed; only the second woman I wouldn't forget and she was right there with me.

In the morning she bathed again and dressed while I watched, gathering her up for the future; what she wore, how she moved, what she said, remembering how we had made love. It seemed likely that I wouldn't see her again and, greedy, I wanted to keep everything I knew of her because I'd heard so many people say that at the end of your life that's all there was.

"Why did you bother?" I asked.

She laughed. "Men always think there has to be a reason," she said. "Sometimes there just isn't one, or if there is it's so small as makes no difference. I'll tell you some other time."

When she was ready to leave she came and stood by the bed. She wore a different dress from the one she'd worn the night before, she must have brought it with her. She said, "You can do me a favour. I've got some pieces to write, a series. Billy told me you have a hideout in the country. You're not there, are you? Why don't you lend it to me?"

I pushed myself up onto my elbows. Time to box clever. "Well . . . how long do you want it for?"

"I don't know, as long as it takes, what the hell does it matter?"

I stopped boxing clever. "Okay," I said, and I told her how to get there, I wrote it down so she wouldn't get lost. Casey Roberts in my house. "Take the road from Littledean to Mitcheldean, second crossroads, turn left. There's an old house, man has it by the name of Phil Barnett, you ask him for the key, there are three tracks going up into the Forest, he'll tell you which one to take. This tour may be finished for me in two or three days, I may have to come home."

"Do what you like," said Casey, "it's your place. Rent?"

I shook my head. She shrugged, taking it for granted anyway. "Suit yourself." She took her bag and left.

As soon as the door had closed behind her I leapt from my bed and ran to the bathroom to look in the mirror. I was laughing.

When I went downstairs later there was no sign of Casey. I had breakfast with the others and didn't say I'd seen her. It was my secret and I didn't want the others to touch it.

Liverpool

We took a couple of hours to load our van and as soon as it was ready Les, Duncan and Duggie drove it away down the road to Heathrow. Billy and I drank some more coffee and then walked across the hotel car-park, lugging our cases.

The black Ford was parked next to the Volvo. The rear door fell open as we approached and Rosser swung himself into view and stepped towards us. We stood amazed, Billy and I, and the wind whipped at us from each corner of the hotel, the warm oil-ridden wind of August. From under the car-park came the drab noise of the motorway, cars and lorries, up country and down. Two other men rose up on the off-side of the Ford, unobtrusive and solid, nicely dressed in suits, carrying briefcases. Ordinary faces from the world's hotel population. They leant against the car, one watched the entrance to the car-park, the other stared up at the unopenable windows of the Fiesta Hotel.

I was pleased to see that Rosser wasn't dead. It was reassuring, though there was no reason why it should have been. Rosser looked as if all his worries were over and he had slept well and long. His clothes were clean and his blond hair shone, under its grease, as black as a beetle, not a hank of it protruded from the hard surface and not a wisp of it was allowed to flutter in the air. Seeing Rosser was like being rescued in the nick of time. Billy smiled.

We threw our cases onto the roof of the Volvo and the three of us leant against it. I took the chance to study Rosser's friends. If they were hit men, then they were uncatchable. Once their job was done they would need only to drive to the nearest hotel, sit down and disappear into the wallpaper. They must have been very valuable. They stood relaxed, their briefcases held oddly across their chests. Then I saw why. The briefcases were slit open at each end, inside was clipped an automatic.

"They told us you were dead," said Billy.

"They say things like that," said Rosser. "Don't you believe them, I'm not going to."

"They pretended to kill me a couple of days ago, the full

Gestapo job, I expected a bullet in the brain and got egg on my face. The way I felt afterwards they might just as well have killed me."

"I didn't say it would be easy," said Rosser. "Nasty does have a certain flair." He chuckled like an academic admiring a friend's mistake.

"You killed those two informers, didn't you?"

Rosser looked towards the Ford. "I had a little help from my friends," he said, "and they're only here on tourist visas."

Billy was shocked. "You live somewhere else," he said and shook his head.

"No, Billy, it's the same place you live, the same place."

"They thought I'd killed the front men."

"No they didn't," said Rosser, "that's just what they said."

"We beat up the coppers afterwards, pushed their car down a hill and put a match to it, did it make the news?"

"Don't be romantic, Billy, they kill that kind of information stone dead."

"It's incredible, I mean they do what they like."

Rosser gave his harsh laugh. "And who's to stop them? There's no one to know what they do day to day except me and others like me, and we're never asked."

That quietened Billy for a while and we listened to the traffic. At last Rosser said, "I've spoken to Nasty on the phone, he was very angry. He didn't like what I did but he has got to deal with us now."

"What did you say?"

"I told him that we wanted a hundred thousand out of it, anything over the top he could have. I didn't tell him why I wanted the money, but who needs a reason for money?"

"No one," said Billy. "What did Nasty say to that?"

"He said he wasn't stupid nor was he the Red Cross. This time he didn't have any choice. The Bunce was in a position where it needed cash in a hurry. He would have it and he didn't care what happened to us. He didn't give an inch."

"So killing the two informers achieved nothing?"

"I wouldn't say that, he hasn't got the same freedom of manoeuvre now, he's got to come through you."

Billy swallowed. "I'm not sure that cheers me up," he said. "So what happens?"

"Well, I slowed him down a bit, I told him the American Trade was involved in your protection. He didn't like that at all. Even the Bunce wouldn't want to get involved with that end of the market."

"How was it settled?"

"It wasn't. We just stopped talking. He wanted to go away and think, it was the old stand-off on the phone. Don't worry, Billy, I've arranged to meet him at the Stardust, after your last show. Believe me, Billy, don't worry, we're nearly there."

"Yeah," said Billy, turning his face to me so that I could watch the blood fall out of it. "Nearly where?"

DAYS 30–34

CHAPTER NINETEEN

The Last Show

We were back at the Stardust Hotel, where we'd begun, and it was the last show. "Exuberance," Max kept saying, his fat hands holding the word up in front of his face as if he'd unfurled a banner: "Exuberance."

He was determined that everyone should know what Morley had achieved in a month and he was assembling the kind of audience that could help him, just as he had at the beginning; men and women from the press, television and radio, British, American, European. And to entertain them, he ordered Billy to invent a brand new circus.

He wanted drum-majorettes marching through the hotel, strolling players singing "Greensleeves" in the galleries, archers dressed as Robin Hood and Will Scarlet to swing on ropes from balcony to stage. There was to be a fire-eater on stilts in the foyer, a sword-swallower, a coconut-shy and a merry-go-round as well. Once again, green branches and flowers would decorate hotel doorways and columns and every waiter and waitress was to be dressed in a medieval jerkin with the letter "M" sprayed across it in multi-coloured tinsel.

"I want everyone to sing the Morley hymns on the last night," Max told us, "performers, technicians, hotel staff, all of you, so you'd better learn the words."

Every day was the same. As soon as breakfast was over Max stood on a chair in the restaurant and told us how he had shaped the next twenty-four hours. Every day a new idea dropped hot from his brain like a bowl of soup out of a vending machine. We were to have trumpeters announcing every act, an armoured knight on horse-back riding through the tables, an eighty-voice male choir from Wales and a Scottish dance troupe with pipers. Max's assistants got no rest. Wherever I went in the hotel I found them running. Every time I opened a lift one of them pushed by me, going in or out, up or down. Their bleepers bleeped and their walkie-talkies talked. They ran all the way and I ran too, just as fast as everyone else.

The new show that Max had given us to put together had been mounted at the Magic Lantern studios on Clapham Common. It had meant a lot more work and a lot more staff; new designs, new slides, new tapes, more machines. We spent hours shouting into phones and their mouthpieces were always warm and dripped with spit. We ate slides, we slept slides. We repainted the set and revarnished it. The moat was inspected for leaks, the church was given brighter windows. We pulled the Morley Dawn up and down a thousand times until Max was satisfied. As the show drew nearer Billy brought in staff from the studios and he hired more. People tramped about the hotel, each one on an errand. The work ground us down; we were too tired to eat and too hungry to sleep and alcohol was the only way to break the circle.

And still Max built his show, adding something to it every minute. During all those nights and days on tour Max had been constructing a monument to his own achievement. When Magic Lantern had driven on to the next venue Morley Pioneers had been left behind to visit the new Instructors in their homes, delivering samples, meeting more people. It was an organisation that had been designed to work; the Pioneers were there to make sure it did.

Photographers had followed the Morley men everywhere, so had film crews and sound recordists. Graphs had been drawn and there were shaded maps. Certificates of merit were framed for presentation, extra speeches recorded and there were newly-minted words for the Professor to boom out from his crag. This was The Show and Magic Lantern put it together in three days, and Max bustled and strangled and commanded and was supremely happy because Freddie and Ruth Beckenbauer were coming over to help spread the Morley word like golden American butter on our dull English bread.

I hardly saw Billy to talk to during all this preparation and toil. We had no time to think of the Bunce or to think of anything. Billy was ill; he hadn't been right since the picnic. He swallowed tranquillizers and pep-pills, mixed, like jujubes, and he carried a magic bottle in each hand. His face looked as diseased as an overnight fungus, a grey puff-ball on a stalk, and although he kept going and did the work the stuffing had gone, he was trailing sawdust everywhere.

And then it was the run up to the show. We had a dress-rehearsal and all the bits fitted. In the late afternoon of DAY 34 Max finally went for his bath and the rest of us went backstage for a meal, our last chance to eat.

I was alone at the table to begin with, watching the waiters bring food and drink. It was dark there, only two yellow working lights hung from the scaffolding gantry. The electricians came, the riggers, laughing and talking with their girls, the extras from Billy's studio, everyone assembled and organised by Fran. There were about forty of us, tired, but moving easily in our own sweat. I felt protected in that blackness and it reminded me of a month's filming I'd once done in a coal mine. A special comradeship had formed between the miners and the film unit, as we'd worked together in the powdered stone-dust, eating gritty sandwiches and breathing in the smell from the gob where we went to crouch and crap. Those back-stage banquets had the same feel, there were the same faint beams of light catching the corners of eyes and faces and they made us all handsome, all friends.

Above us as we ate loomed the ultimate surprise; a huge statue of the Professor, flown in from New York, three times life-size, one finger pointing to the ceiling, one hand holding the books of wisdom as he strode, in a loose suit, across a hemisphere. As the dawn went up this time we would unveil the Professor, a gift from the parent company over the ocean to the fledgling organisation in Market Harborough. He was a statue carved with skill out of a material that would outlive stone and outlast bronze, his surface was smooth and metallic. As Max said, "You can't beat fibre-glass for that ever-living work, and you can air-freight it anywhere in the world, economically too, and just three men can lift it."

Ten minutes before the show. Behind the set I had about a hundred people to shuffle into order and I had two "wingers" to run my errands; two blond secretaries from Billy's office. The drum-majorettes leant against the back wall smoking, and the bandsmen folded their arms or drank beer from brown bottles. Performers crossed from right to left, chatting, and I followed them, the long lead trailing from my earphones. I carried a clipboard.

"I'm bringing the grams up," said Billy down the wire, "coffee's gone, liqueurs are out, the last waiters are leaving . . . Okay, fellas stand by, Les, house lights. Duncan, Duggie, Mike, here we go . . . let's have those trumpeters in position, Mike. Light them, Les, stage left, stage right. Okay, fellas, it's back on your heads."

We were there, into the last show.

There was more entertainment than information this time. It was going to be relaxed and friendly, lots of fun, lots of noise. Gradually we eased our way into the programme and began to unwind. We each had a bottle of spirits and I began to drink mine. The slides went through, the tapes spun and the live acts got on and off when I told them to and I was right. Troubadours wandered amongst the tables and the dancers followed. The show rolled on over the edge and took everyone with it, like an avalanche.

About two-thirds of the way through Max made his speech. I got him on to a fanfare and he stood in front of the church and told Freddie and Ruth and the others how complete a success the tour had been. He was cheerful, confident, cool and brief; it would not be many years, I told myself, before Morley was the multi-national corporation that Max yearned for it to be. When he came off-stage the audience got to their feet and applauded him for five minutes. As I helped him down the steps he smiled at me, directing that obscene wedge of light right into my eyes. "Great show, Mike," he said and strode away leaving me with a feeling of pride in my heart. That was Max's strength and that was my stupidity. I had to shake my head and remind myself that I was there for the wages and nothing more.

We were about a quarter of an hour only from the end of the show when it happened. I was moving the Professor's statue into position when one of my wingers touched me gently with her outstretched hand, at the same time I heard swearing in the headphones and became aware of an increase in audience noise. I glanced at my assistant and she jerked her head at the screen, her eyes wide. Everyone back-stage, I knew it without looking, was staring upwards.

It was a good picture, nicely lit and sharply focussed and it ran across the five screens in full colour, thirty feet by six, and it showed a half-erect penis with a woman's mouth round it. I heard a clatter as someone in the auditorium dropped a tray of glasses and Max buzzed on the line from the back of the room.

The last part of the show was pulsed but Duncan had an override button.

"Pump it up, Dunc, pump it up." Billy was shouting but Duncan had already triggered the hand control. The next slide came up as per script and the next, and the next. The commentary was right too and the audience noise subsided. We waited.

The second picture came just when we had convinced ourselves there would be no more. Duncan pumped it off immediately but it was followed by another and that caught him on the hop. The commentary didn't help either. "The biggest operation this century," said Max's recorded voice, "and yet reminding us of Nature's part in everything we do." Duncan got it off the screen but the audience had seen it and there was laughter.

"Cut the power," shouted Max, but none of us answered. We were still watching, motionless, waiting for each slide to drop down.

"Stand by," said Billy, "Statue, Mike, get everyone to take positions." Billy was saying the right things but his voice was high, near to a strange hysteria.

Nasty had not sabotaged the whole sequence. We had seen three slides and there were only three more to come, but, shot from a wider angle, they showed us more of the participants. Duncan got them off the screen as quickly as he could but it would have been obvious to anyone who knew them that they were pictures of Billy and Eunice. Billy kneeling and Eunice crying in that hotel room in Nottingham. In the background were the men watching, their faces painted out. There was scattered applause from the audience and one or two shouts.

"The bastards," said Billy, "the bastards. How did they do it?"

Billy's question was certainly to the point. It was clear that Nasty had shot the slides and planned the substitution but only someone with special knowledge could have put the slides into the right carousels, and only someone working for Magic Lantern could have had that knowledge. It could have been any of us, we were all bribable, but I was the most likely, the carousels had always been my responsibility.

The music tape became more grandiose and we worked our way towards the end. The slides filled the screen, all of them as scripted now, faster and faster; scenes showing the Morley show on the road, seminars, dinners, the new recruits, everyone singing, everyone holding hands. The music rose and, just when we thought it was over, Nasty slipped in his last slide and not one member of the audience seemed to notice it, but we did, all of us. It was a close-up of Jim's body under a blood-stained sheet in the morgue. We knew it was Jim because they'd uncovered his cowboy boots so we could tell.

And that was it. Five slides grew on the five screens and showed the dawn. Billy gave Les the word and up came his massive barrage of light. I was still staring at the spot where Jim's picture had been and I nearly missed my cue. I ran over to the band-master. "Make lots of noise," I said, "lots of it."

"Joyous row," he said.

"Yes, and keep the drum-majorettes marching for as long as you can." I shouted across to the leader of the choir. "Give it everything, everything you've got."

Now I wanted exuberance, just as Max did, not for his sake but for Billy's. Then I went to the statue and in the middle of a huge commotion we wheeled it on.

We could have carried it of course, three or four of us, but that would have given the wrong effect. Max wanted it to look heavy, he wanted us to heave it on, technicians, stage hands, singers, dancers, everyone, and we did what he asked, some of us pulling on ropes forward and some pulling on ropes backwards so that the statue did not move too quickly or seem too light. Others sat on the plinth and did nothing, but their weight alone prevented the Professor from toppling over.

As we appeared on stage the music surged to meet us. From the balcony a hundred hands threw flowers down to the tables and onto our heads, garlands too, made from pink and waxy petals, flown at the speed of sound that day from the Pacific Islands. The audience snatched at the odourless blooms and sang the Morley hymns and cheered and laughed and clapped. When the Professor was centre stage we stood close to him and raised our arms and placed the garlands around our necks, and the audience swarmed up to join us on the set; Morley Pioneers, drunken reporters, little dumpy women from Head Office, freeloaders, there wasn't room for them all and they scrambled and fought to gain a foothold, to get nearer to the Professor, to touch him. And they were crying, most of them, their tears streaming across burning cheeks, eyes mad, alight, aflame; believers spinning in their own delirium like dervishes carrying Ozymandias to the temple.

Then the music came to an end and we heard a trumpet and we stood still and applauded ourselves; we on stage applauded those below, and those below cheered us above, and the noise went on and on as if meant to go on for ever.

I had not dreamt of such exuberance, it made the audience forget Nasty's slides, it nearly made *me* forget; but when the clamour had diminished a sadness remained, the sadness of Jim in Newcastle morgue. There was no one to go to for comfort, no one to tell, no one even who would understand what had happened except the very man who had sabotaged Magic Lantern and devised his own dreadful images to mock our impotence.

DAY 34

CHAPTER TWENTY

The Deal

There were twelve magnums of champagne in ice-buckets on a trolley back-stage and, when it was all over, that was where we went. It was a sad champagne, the same brand they give to the losing side at a cup final. A lot of noise still came over from the audience; they had gathered in groups and they filled each other's glasses. Many of them stayed seated at the tables talking, others went to the bars. The Morley Office had taken over the top floor of the hotel and there was to be an all-night party. We had been invited too, all forty of us, but now we didn't know. None of the Morley people came back to share a drink.

Billy sat on a camera-case under the rostrum and drank from a bottle. "Magic Lantern is dead," he said, "Magic Lantern is dead."

"Someone must have done it while we were eating," said Duncan. "It was my fault, I should have stayed with the projectors."

Billy shook his head. "Who was to know?"

"How bad is it if Max doesn't pay?"

"I'm overdrawn forty grand, that's about what he owes me."

"All that goddam work," said Duggie.

"Yeah," said Billy, "all that goddam work."

We stood around not knowing what to say, depressed; for us the show had been destroyed. One of Max's runners popped his head round the set, looked at Billy and then went away.

Les poured some more champagne. "It'll be all right, I mean Max will come round, it wasn't our fault."

"He had Freddie and Ruth watching that show," said Billy, "and it made him look a fool and there's nothing more guaranteed to put him in a killing mood. I've got to be dead." He saw the worry on our faces. "It's all right, I'll pay you all off before the bank knows what's happening."

It was pretty unhappy back-stage and after a while I put down my glass and went to look for Fran, Billy needed her right then. I scouted all the way through the hotel; the auditorium, the bars and right into the rooms where the Morley party was to be held. There was no sign of her. Fran had always known about Eunice, but that didn't mean she would have liked seeing Billy and her on our super-screen ripple. She must have gone straight home.

On my way back, passing through reception, I saw something that scared me more than anything else I'd seen during those three weeks. I saw Nasty and Max sitting in a corner with a pot of tea between them and the sight of those two men talking at the same table made me sick.

Billy was on his own when I got back to him. Duncan and Duggie were dismantling the projectors and Les was taking the lighting apart, the electricians were disconnecting the cables.

"I couldn't find Fran," I said. Billy just sat. After a while I added, "I didn't switch carousels, Billy, I didn't." He shrugged.

The riggers began to pull the set apart, shouting as they worked. The auditorium sounded empty now, except for waiters and waitresses, folding the tables, stacking chairs. Billy and I waited.

We did not wait for long. I don't know what I expected from a meeting between Nasty and Rosser, perhaps I imagined a scene from a TV series; cops and robbers, tough justice American style, *High Noon*. It wasn't like that at all. It was calm and gentle, though the violence was there all right, like it's always there, coiled and quiet, like a python digesting a goat.

I sat with Billy at the top end of the trestle table where we'd eaten. It was still littered; broken glasses, plates of steak sandwiches gone cold, puddles of champagne, blobs of mustard with cigarette stubs leaning out of them. I looked up to see Nasty appear at the far corner of the set, stepping like a boxer round the crouching figure of one of the riggers who was working there. He was followed by his four men but they didn't even have their hands in their pockets. I glanced to the balcony expecting to see Rosser and his men, expecting to see guns. "Okay, Fat Man, this is where you get yours." Nothing of the sort. Rosser was there, certainly. He had his leg over the balcony rail and it swung easily as he waited. As soon as he saw Nasty he got up and went out of sight, going for the staircase that would bring him down to us, right behind where we were sitting. Nasty's men went to sit stage left, out of earshot but within range. I looked up to the balcony again. Rosser's two American friends were talking to Les now, smiling.

Nasty sat down a few seats away from me and Rosser came in through the door behind us. He took a bottle of champagne from a bucket, two clean glasses, showed the label to Nasty and then poured. None of this seemed real. Round about us the set came down. The riggers hammered and bellowed and shouted and swore. It was all over.

Billy raised his head from his hands and saw the two men. "So," he said, but he wasn't really interested in them. All he could think about were those slides and what they'd done to his show, what they'd done to Magic Lantern.

Rosser sat down and sipped his champagne but Nasty ignored the wine. His big round face gleamed in the down lights, he cupped his right fist in his left hand and laid them both on the table, carefully, like he was carrying an ounce of nitro-glycerine. It was easy to see that he hated Rosser.

"Twice," said Nasty, "is too much, Rosser. Not today, Rosser, but soon. You know I don't let things go."

"Today," said Rosser, "let's talk about today, let's talk about the money."

"Very well," answered Nasty. "I have a pressing need for cash, I need the reward money and I'm going to have it."

"Your two informers are dead, you won't find any more to take that kind of risk. The Trade knows me."

Nasty didn't listen. "The word is out on you, Rosser, you'll be dead within the week."

Rosser smiled. "We're talking about today . . . let us not lose our tempers. Your two front men are dead, the reward has to come through Billy."

There was silence and Nasty shook his head.

Rosser sighed. "Billy and I will settle for fifty thousand each, the rest is yours. That could be a great deal, there could be another hundred thousand in it."

"I want all of it," said Nasty, "I'm under pressure."

"I'm under more," said Rosser. I expected him to look up to the balcony but he didn't. I did, and the two men were still talking to Les.

"Are you all right, Billy?" Duncan and Duggie were leaning over the rail of their rostrum. Billy waved a hand but they stayed watching, pretending that there was something they could do to help but there was nothing. Only Rosser and Nasty could decide.

Nasty tried another tack and the discussion opened in a different direction. "Whatever happens," he said, "that slob is not getting a penny." He meant Billy.

"I did a deal," said Rosser flatly.

"You did a deal." Nasty laughed.

There was a crash and part of the set came down and we could see through into the auditorium. The riggers were making a pile of branches in front of the stage, the moat was already stacked in its sections and Max appeared, walking towards us through the tables. He didn't have a single runner with him.

Billy touched my shoulder, surprised. "I don't want him getting into this," he whispered to me, "get rid of him, keep him away."

"Don't be stupid," I said, "how can I?"

Billy leant towards Nasty, speaking to him before Max could hear. "You cut me out of what's mine," he said, "and I'll spend the rest of my life seeing that you are brought out in the open. I've enough contacts in the press."

Rosser smiled and Nasty laughed again.

"You're bankrupt, Billy, and you've got no muscle. There isn't a newspaper man alive who'd risk his neck for anyone, let alone you. You just shut up and do as you're told."

Max sat down behind Billy, elbows on the arms of his chair, finger-tips pressing against finger-tips, making a prayer house.

Nasty went on. "You don't figure, Billy, I've got a copy of your bank account here." He threw it over. "I could wrap up Magic Lantern tomorrow."

Billy spoke to Max without looking at him. "You'd hold my cheque, wouldn't you, because of those slides, even though the money's mine?"

Max pursed his lips and Nasty said, "I could ruin the Morley operation in Britain and that man knows it."

Max shifted his plump behind. "Morley is vulnerable, like everything. I didn't ask for this, Billy, I couldn't carry the wrong kind of publicity and that kind of publicity is easy to manufacture. Slow down, Billy, you're being greedy."

"He means," said Nasty, "that his kind of business wouldn't bear close scrutiny, it is also easy to sabotage."

"I'll sue you for my money, Max," said Billy.

"Yes," said Max, "of course. You'll remember the let-out clause in our contract about serious faults in the presentation. Today qualifies, Billy. By the time my lawyers had finished, you wouldn't be allowed to drive an electric milk-float."

Max waved a hand and Billy was dismissed from the argument, but Max hadn't finished talking. He glanced at Rosser's Americans and then turned to Nasty.

"I know whose interests those gentlemen represent," he said. "Next year my company goes public, a lot of new money will be coming into Morley, American money, and I don't want to upset those interests. It's a complicated situation but I'm sure that Billy will allow himself to be guided by me here. Whatever happens, a solution must be found that satisfies us all—especially, as far as I am concerned, the two gentlemen on the balcony."

After that there was nothing left in Billy; he leant back in his chair and gave in. All he could do was listen.

Everything seemed right for Nasty. He turned then to Rosser as if to the main business on an agenda.

"Rosser," he said, "I have learnt that the Heathrow job was yours. I know now why you want this money and why those men up there are over from America."

Rosser had good control. He nodded once and let Nasty talk.

"I can get rid of you, Rosser, when I like. You have no muscle here, either. I can do a straight deal with the Americans."

Rosser took some more champagne. "What you say is true," he said calmly, "more especially since you seem to have removed Billy from the equation, but there's a snag as far as you are concerned. I have convinced my two friends that the only thing stopping me getting those four men out of prison is you. If I leave this table in anger they'll put a bullet through your brain before you get to your feet. I'm afraid there is no time for you to rearrange the game."

There was a long silence and I took some champagne myself. Rosser leant back in his chair and crossed his ankles. Nasty opened his right fist and looked at the palm of his hand to see if the explosive was still there. "If they shot me," he said, "what do you think my four associates would be doing?"

Rosser shrugged. "This kind of talk will get us nowhere,

will it? If you want to keep it quiet then you've got to do a deal."

There was a longer silence. Another huge section of the set came down and more of the auditorium became visible. An electrician threw cables down from the overhead lighting gantries and Les was still talking to the two Americans. At last Max came to stand at the table and rested his hands there, keeping his arms straight, weight forward as if he were addressing a board meeting.

"It really is quite simple," he said, "there is a way out, a short term solution if not a long term one. The main thing is to get round the corner. In the interests of a deal, you will have to suspend your dislikes until the business is concluded. You want the money and you want the four men out of wherever they are."

"Wandsworth Prison."

"*Out* of Wandsworth and into America." Max looked at Nasty. "That's got to be easy for someone with your contacts." Max turned to Rosser. "And if your men come out you don't need the money to arrange such an operation with any other organisation . . . really, you could settle this hash without any unpleasantness at all." Max sat down abruptly. I was surprised there was no applause.

Nasty didn't hesitate. He took several cheque books from his pocket and spread them out on the table like he was playing stud poker. "I agree," he said to Rosser, "because I am in a hurry. Afterwards I will see to it that you are killed, just as soon as I can make the arrangements."

He spoke like a man confirming the date of a family party. Max beamed. Nasty finished writing his cheque.

"I shall need all the money," he said. "I am estimating, for the time being, a reward of a hundred thousand pounds, any subsequent monies made available by the insurance companies must come to me. I'll take fifty thousand today, the remainder when the men come out. I shall hold them until the money comes through."

Rosser nodded and Nasty blew on his cheque, though there was no need to; he'd written it with a gold ball-point.

"The reward has been cleared by the companies involved and as Loss Adjustor in this case I have made out a cheque for a hundred thousand pounds to Mr. William Jay, who gave information which led to the recovery of property stolen from Heathrow Airport in August of this year." He handed the cheque over to Rosser who looked at it and then passed it on to Billy.

Billy took it and held it in his big fingers, tenderly, like it was a fragment of a Dead Sea scroll. I peeped at it, it was wonderful: "Pay William Jay the sum of . . ." There it was, in letters and figures, "A Hundred Thousand Pounds Only." Only! The nearest Billy had ever been to real money. Above us, leaning out from the gantry rail, Duggie pushed a whistle of wonderment through his teeth. Billy stared at the cheque, he didn't move.

"I want your men out of the country as soon as you get them," said Nasty and Rosser inclined his head. His champagne was flat now but he sipped it nevertheless. Max laid his cherub's hand on Billy's shoulder and said, "Billy, make out a cheque to Mr. Rosser."

Billy looked at Rosser and Rosser shrugged by way of apology. There was nothing to be done. Billy was caught in the middle of a straight business deal and there was no way out, but there was one thing he could do and he did it. He knocked Max's hand from his shoulder, "I don't write a damn thing," he said, "until you make out a cheque to Magic Lantern for what I'm owed."

Max hesitated, he glanced at Nasty and Nasty hesitated too. Rosser banged down his glass. "Do it," he said, "Billy's been screwed enough. It wasn't his fault the show went sideways, he's done the work."

Nasty nodded and Max wrote his cheque; "I'll make it out for thirty-five," he said. "We can do the fine adjustments later."

"All right," said Billy, and took Max's cheque.

"You're sentimental," said Nasty. "Does it matter if Magic Lantern goes broke?"

"I don't know," said Rosser, "it might."

Billy took out his cheque book. "What initials?"

"Rosser, Richard Rosser."

I watched Billy write: "Pay Richard Rosser the sum of One Hundred Thousand Pounds." He tore the cheque away at the stub and slid it across the table to Rosser, who verified the date, the amount and the signature. When he was satisfied he folded it carefully in half and tucked it away neatly into the back of his cheque book which lay on the table by his glass. He held out his hand for Nasty's pen.

"Make it out to the Vauxhall Insurance Company," said Nasty.

"Fifty thousand pounds," said Rosser, and began to write.

There was a loud report and a shout of happiness came from the riggers as another section of the set fell down. The noise rose about us now, as they began to stack stage-weights and French stays ready for transportation.

Rosser held up the oblong of paper and looked at it: "The other half on completion," he said.

"I've never fallen down on a contract," said Nasty, "you know that. If you don't, you will."

Rosser held onto the cheque, waving it dubiously, like a child greeting royalty with a pennant. "I hope that Morley man knows exactly what happened to Billy's slides."

Max flapped his hands. "I'm sure that Morley and Magic Lantern will have no such trouble in Europe."

Nasty snatched the cheque and inspected it closely. "As far as I'm concerned," he said, "Billy can work himself to death."

Rosser stood up. The men on the balcony stopped talking to Les and held their briefcases across their chests, but Rosser smiled and slipped Nasty's gold pen into his pocket. I liked him for that, even though he'd been forced to double-cross Billy.

Nasty picked up his briefcase. "I suggest," he said, "that we all present ourselves at our banks at ten o'clock tomorrow morning and lodge our cheques. These are large sums; if there are any queries then we'll all be on hand, though I'm sure there'll be no need." He turned and walked through the remains of the set and into the auditorium, where his four men rose from one of the dining tables and followed him out. Rosser went out the other way, to the balcony, and disappeared with the two Americans. Max went upstairs to his party and Les stared down at us from the lighting control, pale-faced, winding a black length of cable onto his shoulder. Billy's dream of getting into the club of the rich had gone.

"They don't make it easy, do they?" said Billy, looking at his cheque for a hundred thousand pounds. "The bastards have got it all buttoned up."

I opened another bottle of losers' champagne.

"After two thousand years of civilisation," I said, "it stands to reason that the shits must be somewhere near the top by now."

DAY 35

CHAPTER TWENTY-ONE

The Script

By three o'clock the next morning the conference hall was empty. The set had gone and there was nothing on the carpet but litter and lumber; branches, scaffolding clips, shattered bulbs and drained bottles. At the far end of the room twenty Mediterranean women were working in a line, sweeping our dirt into piles and carrying it away. Tomorrow would be Day One of somebody else's conference.

The pantechnicon had taken Merrie Englande to be loaded into crates for Europe; in Germany the church would become a Rhine castle, in France a Loire château. Duncan, Duggie and Les had driven the van back to Clapham. For them, two weeks' work while they checked through the equipment and got ready to take Morley over the channel. There would be new slides to mount, new tapes to pulse and Max every day. I was well out of it.

Billy and I were walking together around the fringes of the rubbish. We'd talked about the Bunce until there was nothing more to say and we knew there was nothing more we could do. Billy still wanted me to go to Europe. "If it's a question of money," he said.

"It's no good, Billy, have you phoned Fran?"

"She'll be asleep. So you won't come?"

The Script

I whined at him, I was so tired. "Drop me off at Paddington, come on, I can catch the 5:30. I just want to go home."

We'd had the car brought round to the front entrance and it was waiting for us on the concrete pad. The sky over London was glowing with neon and the motorway noise was steady. A jet dropped on to the airport. Billy stretched his arms above his head and his belly lifted. "Do you know what people pay for a good film script?" he said. "A feature I mean, not the crap we do."

I got into the car. "Lots of money."

"There's no limit, it's what you can get. Anywhere between twenty and two hundred thousand."

"Pounds or dollars?"

"Both, either." He came round the passenger side and shoved me over. "You drive, I'm going to drink."

"Aw, shit, Billy, I won't get home until this afternoon." I remembered then that Casey Roberts was at my place, but I didn't say anything.

Billy ignored me. "So it's right in front of us and we nearly miss it, and we're in the business."

"What?" I asked.

"This bloody story, seen it with our own eyes, the whole Bunce thing, what a script."

I began to drive the Volvo towards London. Billy groped around the floor of the car and came up with a bottle of whisky.

"Don't start again, Billy." He took a big mouthful and swallowed it. He handed the drink to me and I took a small one.

"What a script," he repeated, "it's got everything, but we'll have to jazz it up a bit. You know, car chases in the hotel car-parks, gun fights between us and them while the last show is actually running."

"Don't go over the top, Billy."

"Who's going over the top? I mean, imagine if Nasty had really sabotaged the show: Max crossing the bridge and falling into the moat, stage-flats falling down in the middle of his speech, it could have been hilarious. Imagine Will Scarlet swinging from the balcony and being stopped short of the floor because there's a rope round his neck . . . splat . . . you'd have a corpse on stage. Can't you just see it?"

"Sounds like *A Night At The Opera,* with blood."

"Right, and a real killing in the Lake District, none of that egg business. The two central characters could be men with SAS training . . . you know, retired from the army and just starting their own A-V company."

"It's not a bad idea," I said, "if it was done properly it could be the best thing since *Rififi Chez Les Hommes,* with Jean Gabin."

"Didn't see it," said Billy. "We'll need a good title, 'The Bunce' doesn't mean much to most people. Do you realise that if this took off I could make more money out of it than out of any reward. You only need one script to make you a rich man. A hundred and fifty thousand pounds at least, plus all the spinoffs."

"Great, but don't involve me, I'm not doing any more work for six months."

"That's your trouble, Mike, you're a waster. You've no ambition, no vision. Money is the only way out!" He drank from the bottle, passed it over and I again took a small nip. We were coming into the Cromwell Road extension.

"I'll do a deal with you," said Billy, and I knew then that he must have been making his plans since the meeting with Nasty. "I didn't get the reward so you don't get the thousand pounds I promised, but I'm now into a lot of Morley money again. I'll give you five hundred, over and above your wages."

"I'm not going on the tour."

". . . And while I'm away you rough out a script for 'The Bunce.' When I come back we finish it off together. It's certain to take off. I've got good contacts, you know. You could write it in six weeks."

Ever since I'd told Billy about Stendhal writing the *Charterhouse* in a month and a half, he'd been convinced that anything at all could be composed within the same time-span.

The Script

"I'm not sure about a film script," I said, "though I like the idea. The first producer you show it to will steal it, you know the film business better than I do. It would be better to write it first as a novel, then they've got to come to us for the film rights."

"A book's not easy to get published," said Billy.

"True," I said, "but I know this judy who works at the Bodley Head."

"Oh, yeah, what's that, some kind of a pub?"

You never knew with Billy so I answered him. "A publisher."

"Anyway, do you do the deal with me? Five hundred, that'll keep you another six months in your shack, you'll have twelve months altogether with your wages."

"I couldn't turn that down, Billy. I'll have to tell the Arts Council about you."

"You'll do better than that, you'll sign an agreement."

"Fifty-fifty?"

"You're joking, it's my idea, and I'm paying you five hundred in advance. I'll give you ten percent of what I take out of the book. That's generous."

I was at the traffic lights by Battersea Bridge. It said no right turn but I went anyway. The sky was going grey over the river, it was first dawn I'd seen for about a month. Billy's proposition wasn't bad. I had the writing to do but I'd get a years's freedom out of it. A whole year without working on conferences. "Okay," I said, "ten percent for the book, what about the film script?"

"I'll give you five percent of whatever I make and that's generous too. I'll be writing that script myself."

I accepted.

We came to Clapham Common and I turned left. A little way along and I stopped outside Billy's houses. The common stretched away in front of us and the fields were empty. Billy looked up at Fran's bedroom then back at me.

"You write a thriller, a real thriller, and remember I have the last word. I know you brainy types, you'll slow it down, ruin it. We want something fast moving, speedboats, helicopters, all that James Bond stuff." He offered me a last try at the bottle but I refused. "We're going to have trouble with the ending though," he went on. "We can't have those guys sitting round swapping cheques, there's no mileage in that. You'll have to work out something and I'll have a look at it when I get back. There's got to be a shoot-out. Rosser shoots Nasty, Nasty fatally wounds Rosser but, before they die we get the money—have to be in cash too, there's no drama in a cheque."

"Oh, Billy, it stinks."

"So does Camembert and they swallow it all the time. You get some story down, I'll knock it into shape. I'll do you a screenplay for the first scene too, just to give you an idea of how it should go. I'll start with the robbery, film it just like it happened, documentary style, *Day of The Jackal*. It'll make a pilot for a TV series, incredible!"

It was incredible all right, it was tragic too. Billy was off again, ready to put himself into orbit round another dream.

We got out of the car, pulled our suitcases from the back and went into the house. There might have been twenty people there but they were all in bed and all the lights were on. I phoned for a cab, Billy made a pot of tea and we waited for it to infuse, sitting opposite each other at the kitchen table.

"You know," I said, "I don't think we've been all that smart."

"What do you mean?"

"Well, if you add it all up it's possible that there's no such thing as the Bunce. It might just be a giant con-trick dreamed up by Rosser. He could have organised the whole thing with Nasty, dressed a few heavies up as coppers and then acted it through just to frighten us off. I suspect he did have to spring those four men but, even if he didn't, the money would have been worth it for its own sake. Like he said, a hundred and fifty thousand isn't just money."

Billy stared at me with hatred. "That's ridiculous. There was a robbery, you know, and Jonathan found the Loss Adjustor through normal channels, even if it was Nasty when he got there."

"Okay, that could have been above board. Nasty was the Loss Adjustor, straight too, but that doesn't stop the rest of it being bent. Rosser could have threatened Nasty, or bribed him, made him go through with the scheme. It's a hard combination to beat, violence and money."

"And the two front men, the police informers, they were shot, weren't they?"

"How do we know? You had a telephone call from Jonathan and then Rosser told us about it. We didn't see anything in the papers; that could have been the Bunce keeping it quiet, or it might never have happened."

"We didn't look in the papers, did we? Anyhow, why should Jonathan lie about it?"

"How long have you known him, how much do you trust the guy? It wouldn't cost a lot to buy him, would it? A couple of thousand and the promise of a bullet in the brain. It would buy me."

Billy waved his hand. "Nah," he laughed. "Rosser and Nasty, you could see they hated each other, and what about the police who came to see us at the Stardust first off, Fisher, and those others about Eunice at Birmingham, they couldn't all be in it, it's too far-fetched."

"I don't know; is it? Anyway, they don't have to be in it. The con could have been arranged so as to fit inside and around the legitimate coppers. It was Rosser who advised you to send for Jonathan, wasn't it?"

"What about the police car behind Panurge at Newcastle, the drunken driving charge, that says the Bunce exists."

I poured myself a cup of tea. "Does it? You didn't go down to see the police yourself, you sent Jonathan."

Billy turned pale. I'd slowed him down at last so I smiled and poured him a cup of tea too.

"There's no point in worrying," I said, "there's nothing you can do. If you stop your cheque they'll make Max stop his and you'll be back in the same old village of stony broke."

"Oh, come on, Max wasn't in it, I mean, he wasn't involved."

"He didn't have to be. Nasty got to Max after the show and threatened Morley. If he was working with Rosser he might even have told him what the Mafia would do to the company back in the States if they didn't get what they wanted here . . . we believed Rosser, after all, and Max would always do what was good for Morley, he wouldn't give a monkey's about you or Magic Lantern."

Billy didn't like this new scenario. "You mean Rosser and Nasty are sharing the money, all of it?"

I shrugged. "I don't know, all I've put forward is a hypothesis."

Billy winced at the word. "If the Bunce exists," he said, "if Rosser's story is true, what's to stop Nasty double-crossing him?"

I laughed. "There'd be no point," I said. "Nasty wants the money, Rosser wants the men out of jail or he's finished. They both want it quietly done. If they both go through with the deal they'll each get what they need; anything else can be sorted out afterwards. They won't squabble until it's all over . . . that is, if the Bunce exists."

Billy shook his head and I could see that I'd worried him. I was pleased with what I'd done but I still wouldn't let him off the hook. "Whichever way you look at it the stories fit; Rosser versus Nasty and the Bunce on the one hand; Rosser and Nasty working a con-trick on the other. Come to think of it—for all we know Rosser could be a full-time copper organising his own robberies while his friend Nasty looks after the shop."

With that idea I'd gone too far; Billy looked like he might be sick at any moment. I relented. "Forget it anyway," I said, "too much money's bad for you, Billy, bad for anyone."

He didn't take that seriously at all. "Crap," he said and drank his tea.

The doorbell rang; it was my cab for Paddington. Billy came out with me and we stood on the step. The sun was up now and the taxi-driver stood gazing at the common, his hands thrust deep into the pockets of his jacket. There was a man walking a dog, a few cars went by. It was good just looking at the grass. That's what I was going to do for a year, watch the grass grow.

"You'd be the same as everyone else if you had real money," said Billy. "We all need it, you can't be what you want without it, you can't spread your wings."

"Maybe," I said, "but perhaps I don't need as much of it as you do, that keeps me a little freer, doesn't it?"

What I said didn't interest Billy, he was thinking about himself. "Mike," he said, "do you really think I was conned?"

I sighed. I felt like saying that it was all too likely but a look at Billy's face was enough to make me change my mind. I couldn't say it, not after all he'd been through. "Nah," I said. "I was thinking out loud again, being hypothetical. The Bunce is real, all right. I'll tell you something, though; it would make a better film scripted that way round. You could keep the audience guessing all the way, cutting backwards and forwards between the conners and the conned."

Billy brightened in a second and blood returned to his face. He took my arm and walked with me to the cab. "That really is a great idea," he said. "It could be that Redford-Newman movie all over again, you know, *The Sting*."

"I didn't see it," I said.

He grabbed me by the shoulders, inspired. "I know a man who knows their agent in Los Angeles. We'll have to write it like that: intricate, complicated, to a certain kind of formula. Redford plays me, Newman plays you."

I put my suitcase into the taxi. "I knew a girl called Monique, once, she always said that I looked like Paul Newman . . . from the back."

When the taxi drove away at last Billy was smiling his scrumper's smile again and waving at me from the kerbside—and there I left him, standing on the edge of the common in the cool early air of south London, the Victorian house behind him ablaze with pale light in every room. He looked hopeful, eager, tall and big with his belly leaning out over his belt. Billy Jay. He'd had a hard road to his forty years and the reward must have seemed close that trip, his dreams so near. In the end they had got away, but he stood there, smiling still, ready to go on running. No matter what happened, battered or breathless, Billy would run and keep on running, uphill into the future, when perhaps all he needed was right there behind him, within reach of his hands.

When the taxi had turned its first corner I put Billy out of my mind and thought about me. I was well pleased. I had enough money to finance myself for a year. I was free. I stretched my arms and laughed, so loudly that my driver glanced up into his rear-view mirror. I would take Billy's money all right and spend it, but I was determined not to write his thriller. The truth of what had happened was story enough, straight down the middle, though it wouldn't be easy. The doubts that I'd maliciously sown in Billy's mind were now springing up in mine. Did the Bunce exist?

If it did, I would have to tread carefully. I wanted neither cops nor robbers leaning on me. My only desire was for the quiet life with just enough money in it to pay for rent and food, nothing more. Others could do the running. I would have to compose a disclaimer for the beginning of the book in order to protect myself, something legal, something watertight.

I took out my notebook; it was nearly full but I found enough space in it and tried out a form of words. When I'd finished I leant back and thought about what I really wanted to think about; Casey Roberts in my house. Casey Roberts in the Forest of Dean, it didn't seem possible.

I looked from the cab window and saw Park Lane with its hotels facing the flat green field. There was traffic groaning through the streets and the town was coming awake, the old town that I had once loved but now couldn't wait to leave.

I took up my notebook and tried the disclaimer again, determined to make it perfect; I read it out loud to the taxi-driver, who took no notice:

The Script

In this book, no reference is made or intended to any particular police officer or group of police officers. Nothing resembling "The Bunce" exists in this country, nor is it likely to. This is just a story . . .

I smiled. That would do nicely, and at least it was a start.

The Guardian

FOUR PRISONERS IN AMAZING ESCAPE

Four American nationals, on remand in Wandsworth Prison in connection with last month's Heathrow robbery, made a dramatic escape from custody yesterday afternoon.

The four Americans, a tie-up with the Mafia has been both suggested then denied by the police, were being held in the strictest security, enjoying only one hour's exercise per day, and that at a different time to the more ordinary inmates of one of London's grimmest prisons.

At 3:30 P.M. yesterday, the four detainees and their warders were alone in the exercise yard when a powerful helicopter appeared over the prison flying in from the direction of the nearby railway line. Almost scraping the walls, the helicopter swooped low and then hovered only a few feet above the ground. The four prisoners, who had dealt with their warders the moment the helicopter had appeared in the sky, lost no time in scrambling aboard the aircraft. According to eye-witnesses, the whole rescue lasted no more than two minutes.

"It was amazing," admitted a Wandsworth warder later, "I think we held back initially because the chopper had POLICE written all over it; but then, even if we hadn't hesitated, they'd have still got away. It was so well planned, so fast."

Scotland Yard at first denied that any of their helicopters were unaccounted for; but under pressure, later in the day, a shame-faced spokesman disclosed that a police helicopter, normally kept at the Battersea Heliport, had been stolen. "An inquiry into the incident has begun," he said, but was unwilling to say more.

The Heathrow saga becomes ever more curious. Small wonder that the underworld calls it THIEFROW.

Michael de Larrabeiti was born in Lambeth. He has worked as a documentary cameraman and as a travel guide in France, Spain, and Morocco. In 1961 he was the photographer on the Marco Polo Expedition, travelling four months overland to Afghanistan on a motorcycle. He is the author of three other books: THE REDWATER RAID; THE BORRIBLES, a children's adventure story about London runaways living in derelict houses and cellars, which provoked widespread controversy when it was published in England in 1976; and an autobiographical novel, A ROSE BEYOND THE THAMES. He now lives in an Oxfordshire village with his wife and two children. THE BUNCE is his first novel for the Crime Club.